THE DREAMER

JEAN SWAN

Published by
DARK SWAN PRESS

ISBN: 978-0-6457263-2-9 (Paperback)
ISBN: 978-0-6457263-3-6 (Ebook)

This book is dedicated to the
Valyns —
those brave enough
to be a little different

P r o l o g u e

Children of Light, listen well, for this is a tale of caution...

We know the Dreamers, those chosen by the Entities to bear the gift of Dreaming; their nights filled with visions of what has gone before and what might be in the future.

But why do the Dreamers test each and every child in the spire?

There once lived a boy on the cusp of manhood. He awaited his first Brotherwalk — the annual journey of men through the forests to the other spires in order to take a lover.

He was everything an Alvar boy should be: polite, attentive, helpful, and eager to serve his spire. On the first few nights of the Brotherwalk, the boy camped with the older men before they went their separate ways. He was observed to be sullen, withdrawn. Some caught him murmuring to himself. Thinking him simply nervous for his first Brotherwalk and not wanting to shame him, the men let him be. They parted ways, and he was left alone in the forest.

No one knew where he was until a month later when he arrived at another spire.

He entered the city stained with blood; weapons drawn. Those who rushed to his aid were slain before they could voice concern. The boy turned his eyes upwards and stalked into the city. Screams met his path, but silence fell behind him.

Without their able men, who had all left for their own Brotherwalk, the spire was defenceless. The visiting brothers did their best to subdue him, but in the time it took, scores lay dead in a bloody swathe of destruction.

They captured him instead of ending his life, their desire for answers burning greater than their vengeance.

The error was realised when he was returned to his spire and examined. An untrained Dreamer had been released into the world. His power, left unchecked, had driven him mad.

For the gift of Dreaming is both a blessing and a curse. It is easy to confuse nightmares for threats when your sleep is plagued by constant alternatives of reality. For the lapse of vigilance by the Dreamers of one spire, the people of another paid the highest price.

So, heed the warning. Dreams are serious. Lies are dangerous.

Anyone, no matter how meek or meagre, can bring destruction upon us all.

I

Beneath the city, tucked within the colossal roots of Ena, the pools of Light glowed softly in the evening darkness. In the shallows, two souls entered the world side by side; mothers clutching hands as they supported each other through the ordeal of birth.

The first child, a girl, wailed loudly as the air of the outside world hit her skin. Her objections at the disturbance of being born rang loudly throughout the minds of the spire, and her mother pulled her close, whispering soothing words. The midwives hurried forward to tie a gemstone amulet around the child's ankle. The moment the stone touched the child's skin, the cries could only be heard by the ears of those nearby.

The second child followed some moments later, as though following the cries of the first. Recklessly, he appeared, his mother crying aloud as some of her pain leaked past her carefully erected mental barriers. For a moment, the whole spire felt her suffering.

The boy stared up at his mother and was silent. The sense of his stunned confusion was quickly wiped from the minds of the spire as an amulet was tied to his ankle too.

The mother of the boy collapsed on the floor of the pool, the Light swirling around her. A midwife offered the boy to his mother, but she shook her head. The mother of the girl reached out for the child instead.

"I will hold him."

The midwife reluctantly surrendered the boy, and the woman settled the two small beings on her chest.

"Welcome little one," she murmured into the head of the boy. "This is my daughter, Valyn." She turned to the boy's mother, now being helped to her feet by the midwives. "What will you call him, Apprentice Speaker?"

"You name him, Roshin," the Apprentice Speaker replied, hobbling from the pool. The midwives cloaked her in a robe, and she pulled it closed around her. "He was a mistake anyway."

Without looking back, she left her son in the arms of another.

"You're not a mistake little one," Roshin whispered to the boy. "Let's call you Theren for now, until she is ready to find a name for you herself."

The two infants nestled against her soft skin and she smiled. Two new lives, born only a minute apart, lay skin to skin. As they would come to learn, their moments together would be plentiful over the coming years.

It was a sad fact of fate that life would conspire to pull them apart.

Theren felt his bones rattle as the snared beast roared.

He had no time for fear, no time for doubt, as the Hunt Master spoke in his mind.

Now.

Theren felt the presence of the eight other Hunters hidden among the trees and undergrowth below, the urge to act thrumming through them simultaneously. From his place on a low branch of a tree, Theren pulled back on his nocked arrow, imbuing it with his Light, and let fly. Together, the other Hunters did the same. A synchrony of silver-blue streaks shot towards the creature, like falling stars with deadly intent. The beast — all muscular arms and thick, black fur — roared again as every arrow found a mark. It whirled in place, unsure where to focus its rage.

Theren slung his bow back over his shoulder and launched from his branch to another lower down before gracefully leaping to the ground.

Hunt Master Feldan stepped forward to draw the beast's attention, facing the creature with his great-spear; a long, glowing shard of crystal. All their weapons were fashioned of the same material, including Theren's glinting bow. Feldan forced the butt of the over-sized weapon into the ground beside him, leaning against it and tilting it towards the beast, who was still flailing wildly in the snare, pulling arrows from its thick hide.

Now. Draw his attention to me.

Hunt Master Feldan spoke in their minds again, and the two closest Hunters joined him, one standing on either side. In unison they lifted their arms, palms outward, and white-blue flames erupted from their hands. It had the desired effect, drawing the attention of the beast, who now had something on which to focus its rage.

While the monster was distracted, a Hunter near the snare pulled out a long-knife. Theren sprinted to the tree behind the Hunt Master and scaled it to sit on the lowest branch, drawing his bow and aiming at the beast once more. It roared again, its silver eyes focused on the Hunt

Master and the flame-throwers standing beside him. The monster was the height of two men, with long arms that allowed it to amble along on its knuckles. Each roar exposed scythe-like teeth ready to shred anyone who got too close.

Any fear Theren felt was buried deep, and he didn't sense any from the others — not even Hunt Master Feldan who, as their leader, would deliver the killing blow.

Set it loose. Contingencies in place. Feldan's voice was a steady stream of words in his mind.

They had all done this before; the hunting band shared an unwavering trust and pride in their role as protectors of the spire. Theren felt the emotions course through him as though he was one of them. One day, he hoped he would belong here, if Hunt Master Feldan thought he was worthy.

He'd prove it today.

The Hunter beside the snare brought the long-knife down in a swift arc, severing the rope, and the beast lunged forward with all the pent-up force of its rage.

Four Hunters stepped out from the under-growth, two on either side of the beast, as it launched itself into a leap, long arms reaching forward. The four Hunters shot glowing ropes from their hands that wrapped themselves around the beast's wrists, holding them in place as its body continued flying forward. The scene unfolded as though time had been slowed. The creature locked eyes with Hunt Master Feldan as it soared across the ground, fangs bared but arms held back by the other Hunters. The glowing lines on Feldan's skin, his ithlyn, flared brightly as Theren felt the man use his power to hold the great-spear in place. Theren's stomach clenched as he watched the creature dive towards their leader; directly at the great-spear stretching out several feet in front of Feldan like a deadly icicle.

The beast's shriek sliced the forest air as its leap was brought abruptly to a halt, the shard piercing through the base of its throat. Feldan's Light flared again as the great-spear was thrust deeper into the soil from the force, the creature almost hanging from the weapon.

Despite the gruesome position, the beast didn't die immediately. It roared and flailed wildly, pulling the Hunters that clung to its arms off their feet. Realising he had a clear shot, Theren pulled back on the bowstring and ignited his arrow with Light. He released. The arrow streaked forth faster and straighter than any natural arrow would, before it lodged itself deep into the beast's skull. The glow within its eyes faded and the creature fell silent, dropping its huge arms to the ground with a loud crash. Theren felt Hunt Master Feldan's approval and tried not to reveal his own burst of satisfaction.

The group's relief was palpable, as though everyone let out a sigh at once. Slowly, the band of Hunters gathered in the clearing as Feldan stepped back from the great-spear, still held in place by the weight of the beast pressing it into the ground.

"Well done, everyone," Feldan spoke aloud as he looked around the party, his approval flickering across their minds. His ithlyn, the slender lines of light that wove along his skin, glowed more dimly now compared to when they had left Starspire two days ago. Out of instinct, Theren glanced down to examine his own ithlyn, feeling depleted himself. He could not see the pale blue lines on his hands and arms for the tight-fitting armour that protected him from finger to toe, but he knew they would be faint. Hunting for days in the forest demanded the abilities that Ena had granted them; the Light from beneath the roots of her great trunk.

"Theren!" One of the Hunters buffeted Theren with his approval, a hint of teasing overlaid. "You stole the killing blow from the Hunt Master!"

Theren glanced at Hunt Master Feldan, his humble apology instant and genuine. Feldan's amusement was a light touch against Theren's mind.

"No need to apologise, Theren. Your courage was deep, and your aim true." Theren looked around the group, their warmth and approval flowing through him even though their faces were expressionless. "We might make a Hunter of you yet — if I can fight off the other Masters!" Feldan added.

Theren's hope danced out from him before he could control it, and a sense of knowing passed among the older men.

"What a time that was," reminisced one of the Hunters. "It feels like just yesterday I was facing my own Choosing and turning myself inside out about it."

The group's mirth flitted over Theren's awareness like it was a mist in the air around him. He fought the urge to smile. At his age, physical expressions of emotion were only appropriate when he was talking to children or wooing a lover from another spire on his Brotherwalk; children were unskilled at mental communication, and citizens of the other spires were not connected to the same Light, their power coming from different Entities.

Theren's stomach sank, and he berated himself for ruining the moment for himself. He was not ready to think about the Brotherwalk, that final hurdle to adulthood. He hushed his mind to hide those shameful thoughts. A boy was supposed to be excited for the event. Every year, all the able men of age left their spires to traverse the forests, visiting the other cities to find lovers and sow the seeds of the next generation. It was not the travel Theren dreaded; it was how one was supposed to know what to do when he arrived.

"Come on, let's get this beast home." Hunt Master Feldan turned to the corpse of the creature lying behind them. "Theren, what can you tell me about this one?"

"It's an ogyr, Hunt Master," Theren replied, casting aside his worries and summarising everything he knew about the creature. He hoped he could impress the Hunters with his beast lore, and he refused to squander this moment by wasting energy on worry.

2

The two babies quickly became toddlers, who became small children. They still wore their blue gemstone amulets, as all children did, to shield their unruly minds from those of the spire. On most days, Theren was left with Roshin as his mother prepared for her role as Speaker. As the two children played on the floor of Roshin's humble home, they babbled and giggled and ran amok — Valyn leading them into trouble and Theren getting them out of it.

On the nights Theren stayed over, the two shared Valyn's bed, curling their little hands around the amulets on each other's wrists. Minds connected, they drifted to sleep entwined in the presence of the other, their dreams shared as though they were one mind in two bodies. Though they did not yet know words to ascribe to the feeling, indeed perhaps words do not exist for such *a bond, it felt as warm as Roshin's whispering hugs and as sweet as the hot drinks they consumed before bed. It was the love of family. Of home.*

The hunting band returned home to Starspire, the city shining through the dim forest like a beacon aglow in pale blue light. Tall pillars of crystal reached upwards beside the colossal trunk of a great tree — the Entity called Ena. The pale blue light from the city gleamed through the shadows of the surrounding forest, where no sunlight penetrated the thick canopy of branches that sheltered those beneath.

To a fresh eye, the towering forest and the crystal towers would have been breathtaking. To those who dwelt within, it was simply home; a haven in the forest of creatures and beasts. Perhaps most importantly, it was the source of their power; the Light that flowed through their bodies and marked their skin with glowing silver lines.

"Greetings, Hunters!" came the welcome of the Head Weaver from under the broad glass arch of the city gate. She and a collection of Weavers eyed the body of the ogyr with delight. "Quite a catch you've brought us!"

The Weavers were the masters of fabrication, supplying the city with Light-crafted materials as well as the more mundane items of leather, leaf, and stone. An ogyr was quite a catch, for much of it had practical use. Its hide was prized for leather and its bones could be crafted into all manner of tools. Theren even knew of a Hunter with an ogyr-fang knife, which was the envy of many of the boys.

"It had gone Light-mad." Hunt Master Feldan made his regret known in the minds of those nearby. "A shame to destroy such a magnificent beast."

"Better it than us," the Head Weaver replied. "As always, you do us a great service."

"Anything for the Weavers and Starspire," Feldan replied.

Though both their faces were impassive, Theren felt a hint of flirtatious energy pass between the two leaders, and he pulled back into himself. Surely the two of them had not meant to share such a thing; romance was forbidden between citizens of the same spire. The others hadn't seemed to notice, but Theren's skill was stronger than most. At times, he caught people's emotions and thoughts with uncomfortable clarity.

One of the many curses of being the Speaker's son; strength ran through maternal lines.

Leaving the ogyr with the Weavers, the hunting band made their way beneath the city to Ena's pools of Light. Though they were called pools, and certainly they were holes in the ground containing a substance that looked like water, they were as much so as gems were rocks. The springs were the source of all power in Starspire, channelling Light from under Ena's roots, through the crystal towers and walkways that weaved around the giant trees surrounding it. Though he had not yet visited the other Alvar spires, Theren knew each contained pools of their own. The men he had seen visiting Starspire on their Brotherwalk had ithlyn in every colour; from the purple of Shadowspire to the East, to the gold of Sunspire farther West.

Theren loped down the stone stairs, wet with moss and dew, following the hunting band as they made their way to one of their favoured pools, glowing beneath thick, twisted roots that lay over the glade like an arbour. The walls were full with ferns and glowing mushrooms, which shone with the pale blue power of the spire. Theren glanced at the ithlyn on the Hunters' faces, emitting only a soft glow after the draining work of the Hunt and the trek home.

Are you done yet?

Theren felt a forceful shove into his mind; a familiar, brash presence enveloping him.

Not yet. I'll come find you soon.

He pushed her out and tightened his mind. There were few people that could get past his mental barriers. With their familiarity, Valyn was one.

The Hunters set their weapons down on the flat, smooth rocks scattered about the glade and began to remove their armour. Theren rested his bow upon the stone, though strictly speaking, it did not yet truly belong to him. Such a possession was only fit for a man, and Theren had not yet crossed that threshold. The looming task of his Brotherwalk came unbidden to his mind once more. A journey to the other spires, his first night with a woman...

Theren's cheeks heated with the thought, and he turned his back on the other men, who were joking both aloud and between their minds. It was a strange conversation for the uninitiated when speech was perceived through both ear and thought. Theren remembered being a young child, still new to the skill of mental communication, and the confusion of trying to follow several conversations at once.

Hunt Master Feldan laid a hand on Theren's shoulder.

"You're emptier than a cask after a Revel, Theren," the Hunt Master murmured. "How are you feeling?"

Inquiries after emotions were words not often heard in the spire; the Light that connected them all meant they were rarely required. Annoyingly, for Theren, they were all too familiar. He supposed the ease with which he perceived others was not received in reverse.

"I'm honoured to have been on the Hunt with you," Theren replied, untying his leather cuirass. "And pleased we've helped the spire."

The sight of the ogyr as the light faded from its eyes swam behind his eyes, pride and regret accompanying it. Theren made an effort to share the thought with the Hunt Master, who returned a feeling of gentle understanding.

"It is a great achievement but also a great burden," Feldan said. "Those who are eager to take the lives of others — even mad forest beasts — cannot be trusted with the safety of our people. For where does the line lie with men such as them?"

Theren glanced at Feldan.

It is not weak of me? he asked in his mind, hoping the other Hunters wouldn't hear.

Of course not, Feldan replied, his presence warm and authoritative. *Such thoughts make you the perfect candidate to take up the mantle of Hunter one day.*

Theren blinked, ensuring his expression remained neutral. It would not do to jeopardise such a lofty compliment by behaving like a child and showing emotion on his face.

Thank you, Hunt Master.

Theren bowed in the Alvar way, pressing his palm against his forehead then turning it outwards. Feldan nodded and returned to the others.

The first Hunter to approach Ena's pool had stripped to his underclothes, little more than a pair of short, skintight pants. Silvery-blue light snaked across his skin, twisting and whirling like vines — his ithlyn. They were clearly visible in the darkness of the glade, but out in the bright light of the city they were harder to see. This man had expended much of his Light on the Hunt, so his ithlyn had lost their lustre.

The talking and joking hushed as he and several others, all near-unclothed, stepped into the pool. As the first man entered the water, his ithlyn flashed brightly; his Light returned instantly to its full potential. Though the man was restored, he descended until he was submerged up to his chin. Reverence was an important part of the ritual.

The other men stepped down, their ithlyn flashing as they, too, were restored. Theren joined them, bare feet padding across the mossy floor onto the smooth stone. How many centuries had feet worn this path, he wondered? The Alvar were as old as the world itself.

As his foot touched the water, a warm, tingling sensation shot through his body like a hot cloth on cold skin. Moving through the Light was like being enveloped in the finest silk. He glanced at his reflection shimmering in the pond, pushing back the long strands of white hair that framed his face. He had his mother's high cheekbones and angular features, so people said. Not eager to think of her, he stepped deeper into the pond until only his face sat above the Light. When he emerged, he was dry. He dressed again, listening to the layers of conversation around him.

"Only a few more days until The Choosing." One of the Hunters addressed him with a mental wave of knowing amusement. "Then you'll be one of us."

Theren felt the rebuke from Feldan, though it was not directed at him. *Don't set the boy's expectations until the Council has sat.*

The Speaker's Council decided where to place those coming of age each year, though only a select few would join a Profession. Theren knew from his mother and sister, the Speaker and the Apprentice Speaker, that the most talented youths were bargained over fiercely by the heads of the Professions.

"I will be content to serve the spire in any way I can," Theren replied humbly to the Hunter.

The sentiment was not quite true; there were some Professions he would rather avoid. The Listeners held little interest to him, their preservation of history and culture far too sedentary for his liking. And, of course, the Dreamers were the least appealing of all. Luckily, they did not wait until The Choosing to take those afflicted with Dreaming, and Theren had already been tested by them. He never remembered his dreams; he doubted he even had them.

Theren walked at the rear of the hunting band as they left the pools, weary legs trudging up the stone steps. He was about to bid the Hunters farewell when a presence in the shadows of an overhanging root filtered into his being. Valyn.

You weren't watching us, were you? he asked. It was forbidden for the men and women of Starspire to bathe together.

A sense of disgust returned to him.

Of course not! Now, are you done?

Theren farewelled his hunting companions. Once they were out of sight, a figure emerged from the shadows. With pale skin, like all Alvar, and white hair she kept short like the boys, Valyn beamed at him like a child. Theren could not help but return the expression.

"Tell me everything about the Hunt!" she said aloud. He felt her envy and desire. None yearned to be a Hunter more than Valyn, though it would never be; women were not Hunters.

His thoughts of rest and a bath were set aside as the two of them made their way up the spire. Theren told her about the ogyr, and she pestered him for every detail. As he spoke, he felt the ache of Valyn's envy; she had been alone for the days of his absence. Seeing him now, recently drained of Light as proof of the excitement of the Hunt, surely only served to fuel her frustration at being denied.

He was weary, but for Valyn, rest could wait.

3

Valyn was missing but Theren knew where to find her.

The children at school had been relentless in their teasing of his friend that day, for reasons that made no sense to him. Valyn had taken off, and no one could feel where she was.

Theren peeked his head into the hollow above the city to see her sitting in the darkness, her arms wrapped around her knees. In her hand dangled a leather cord. Theren knew what she was holding.

"Go away," Valyn grumbled.

Theren vaulted into the huge hollow and used his Light to grow two fern fronds over the entrance, hiding them from the outside world.

"What happened?" he asked.

"Syren said I was as weird as a Dreamer," Valyn mumbled. "And...other things."

She hid her face in her arms, and Theren tossed his hand to throw glittering wisps of light above them.

"Show off," his friend muttered, resting her chin on her forearm. With her hand around the amulet, she was not able to use her Light.

With great effort, he summoned a small breeze, controlling it through the left fern frond.

"Theren's not a show off," he said in a high-pitched voice as the fern waved. "Why, thank you, Miss Fern," Theren said in his own voice again.

Valyn rolled her eyes and nudged him.

"Don't you have somewhere to be?" she asked, a small smile twitching at the edges of her mouth.

"Yes, home," Theren grunted. "Your mother sent me to find you. We're having hot pouches for dinner."

He knew if it weren't for the amulet, he'd feel her excitement. His own mouth watered at the thought. Roshin's leaf-filled pastries were to die for.

After a long pause, Valyn released her legs.

"Fine," she said. She stomped to the front of the hollow. "Move, Miss Fern!"

Though Theren had used half his Light already, he eagerly called back the breeze.

"Hey! Don't talk to me like that!" he squeaked as the fern rustled.

Valyn laughed, and he smiled. All was right in the world again.

Theren and Valyn made their way up through Starspire, along glowing glass streets and past spherical homes, like opaque bubbles floating along the encircling walkways. Bridges arched from tower to tower, linking the crystal city with the enormous trees to hold everything in place. Amidst it all was the colossal trunk and branches of Ena, her bark shot with the lines of Light that connected her with the surrounding forest, just like the ithlyn that scored the skin of those who were born within her pools.

They passed several citizens, who all stopped to greet Theren eagerly. They were barely civil to Valyn, who made no effort to hide her disdain in return. One group they passed greeted Theren with more enthusiasm than all the rest; a crowd of their year-mates who were all facing The Choosing in several days. Theren felt their delight and welcome as they exchanged pleasantries. Long gone were the days of loud jokes, smiles, and claps on the back. From the feeling of excitement emanating from the group, they had been discussing the upcoming Revel;

the celebrations held to send off the men on their Brotherwalk and to welcome the men from other spires who would be staying in the city. Although none of them had experienced the celebrations first-hand, they had felt the chaotic thrill of drunk abandon each year during the Brotherwalk season, as the celebrating adults lost some of their self-control. Soon, however, the topic changed to Theren's Hunt, with everyone hungry for details.

"Of course, the Hunters are going to take you," a pretty girl called Lilithyr said to Theren. "Why else would they have taken you on a Hunt this close to The Choosing?"

Theren felt Valyn bristling beside him. Lilithyr evoked an incomparable fury in Valyn, and he was still uncertain as to why. When they were younger, Lilithyr and Valyn had been close.

"*I* got back from a Hunt two days ago," one of the boys bragged.

"But you didn't kill an ogyr," Lilithyr retorted.

"Looks like we have at least two Hunters on our hands," one of the other girls attempted to placate the boy.

"Pity it's not three, eh Valyn?" Lilithyr's eyes landed on Valyn, where she stood slightly behind

Theren. "It wouldn't be the first thing you've wanted that you can't have."

Valyn took an abrupt step forward and sent a wave of fury at the group, along with a vision of tossing Lilithyr off the edge of the bridge by her long, white hair.

Val... Theren sighed in her mind as he felt the horror from the group. Lilithyr's eyes widened in a child-like display of fear.

"You're a monster, Valyn," the pretty girl hissed. "Ever since-"

"We're going," Theren cut in before Valyn *did* toss Lilithyr off the bridge. He took his friend by the elbow and steered her away from the group.

I don't know why you waste your time with her, Theren, one of the boys called into Theren's mind, putting his arm around Lilithyr to comfort her.

Theren hastened their pace, rapidly putting distance between them and the group, as Valyn's tirade hissed forth. "She's an absolute, Void-spawn, bi-"

"Valyn!"

Valyn bristled at the reprimand. "And thanks for sticking up for me," she said, the sarcasm in her voice as heavy as that she sent from her mind.

"It was just a joke," Theren objected. "You can't take things personally all the time."

"I *can* take a joke! It's just not a joke when it comes from Lilithyr. You don't know the feeling that lies under her words!" Her anger sizzled between them.

"You're one to talk," Theren retorted. "Tell me the last time you let her walk past without thinking some insult at her?"

"She deserves it!"

An overwhelming rush of exhaustion rose through him, and Theren sighed loudly. "Your problem, Valyn, is that you're always angry – but you never do anything to try and make things better."

Theren regretted his words immediately, bracing for a vicious retort, but Valyn did not respond. That was somehow worse, and guilt sat heavy in his stomach. They continued walking in silence. Up they journeyed, past the limits of the spire where the crystal road turned to branches and their steps became leaps as they jumped from branch to branch. Valyn's disquiet beside him was loud; a dark whirl of frustration, betrayal, shame, envy, and some other, deeper feelings he couldn't put a name to. He didn't know what to say about it, nor how to claw back his own cruel words, so he said nothing.

Once out of sight of the spire, they found their favourite haunt; a portion of the upper forest where several trees leaned toward each other, creating a collection of branches that criss-crossed like roads. In the trunk of one of the trees was a huge hollow, which had once been used for hiding in but now contained an illicit stash of weapons.

"I'm sorry," Valyn said suddenly. "I should have kept my mouth shut. And I'm sorry for making you come up here after you just returned. You're tired."

Her apology was direct, but the tentative hope he felt from her was soft and full of doubt, as though she worried that perhaps this time Theren would not forgive her for her temper.

"You've given me an excuse to avoid seeing Mother," Theren reassured, somehow finding his own apology hard to conjure. Instead, he vaulted up to the hollow. He pushed thoughts of his mother far from his mind. It was irrational — simply thinking about someone would not call their attention — but he always felt it was better to be safe than sorry when it came to the Speaker. "I think I'd rather get yelled at by you." He held up a long-knife from the hollow. "Or stabbed, if you're up for it?"

Valyn's grin was accompanied by a rush of relief.

"I think if anyone's stabbing anyone, it's you."

Theren pulled another long-knife from the hollow. Both were wrapped in thin leathers to prevent injury when they sparred. The long-knives had gone 'missing' from the weapons cache many years ago.

"I don't know," he replied, tossing Valyn a weapon. She caught it deftly and spun it around in her hand. "You've left a couple of good bruises on me of late."

Pleased that they had managed to avoid an argument, he leapt down to the branch and positioned himself with the knife outstretched. Though his limbs ached from the days in the forest, he was glad of the distraction to head off Valyn's black mood. Besides, in only a matter of weeks, he would not be here to spar with her at all. Not for months, anyway.

Valyn laughed at him. "Not as many bruises and scars as you've given me over the years."

"What will the brothers from the other spires say when they see them?" Theren teased, regretting it immediately. Teasing each other about the Brotherwalk was something he did with his other friends. Valyn frowned, immediately becoming darker, moodier.

"They'd have to see them first," she muttered, before her mind disappeared from his consciousness. The vacuum of her absence was his warning; she immediately launched herself at him with the blade. Theren blocked his mind, too, to prevent her from reading his next move.

They exchanged blows as he pressed her back down along the tree branch, the muffled thud of the long-knives relentless as he bore down on her. Though he was tired, he was still taller and faster, with years of training that Valyn had been denied.

But none of that crossed his mind as Theren assumed the fighting form named for the rock-cat; nimble-footed as he launched a slashing attack. The Alvar had little need to fight each other with weapons; there were no Alvar wars recorded in the Listeners' histories. And their only enemy, the Void, had been wiped out near a thousand years ago. Now, their duels served only as practice against facing the animals of the forest and to demonstrate one's prowess.

Valyn backed into the tree trunk, a look of determination on her face. She was running out of branch. Leaping backwards, she landed a hand and foot upon the tree, pushing away from it with a flare of her Light. She shot overhead in an arc, slicing towards Theren as she did — a move he only just managed to dodge.

He turned to face her, and she grinned, waggling her eyebrows at him in a most child-like fashion.

"No Light!" he scolded her. "How will you explain when you have to go and restore at Ena's pool?"

A new and sudden presence caught his attention from behind as Valyn's face fell.

"What in the name of Ena are you two doing?"

Theren was buffeted by the force of a reprimand so strong he stumbled backwards slightly. He turned to face the newcomer; his older sister, Ylia, who needed neither posture nor facial expressions to communicate her anger, but used them anyway.

Valyn put her knife behind her back and dropped her gaze to her feet.

"Apprentice Speaker." Valyn sent obeisance outwards along with no small part fear. Theren's own emotion was something far pricklier.

"Ylia. What do you want?" he asked with a resigned sigh.

"Mother wants you," Ylia replied with a flash of irritation. "You didn't come home on your return, and neither she nor I could feel your presence."

People often complained he was hard to sense, but his mother's Light was strong, as was Ylia's. It should have been easy for her to feel him. Perhaps he was blocking more than he realised.

"So how did you find me?"

Ylia raised an eyebrow at him like she was scolding her daughter. Valyn's presence behind him hushed. Of course; he may be hard to find, but Valyn's mind was far easier to sense.

"I shouldn't be surprised about this." Ylia waved her hand loosely at the long-knives. Theren wasn't sure if she spoke to him so expressively because she was a new mother, or whether she simply still considered him a child.

"Don't tell Mother. Please." Theren stepped in front of Valyn. "It's my fault."

"No, Theren, it is *not* your fault." Ylia set her gaze past him, and he felt Valyn wilt. "Judging by the skill I just saw displayed here, this has clearly been going on for some time."

"Please don't tell her," Theren asked again. He sent Ylia a plea of desperation.

"I *should* tell her," Ylia replied, but it was an empty threat. There was plenty Ylia had kept from their mother over the years. Neither sibling was eager to raise the Speaker's ire; there was no way of knowing whether the messenger would bear the brunt of her fury. "Just don't let me — or anyone else — catch you at this again."

Ylia left, leaving the echo of her disapproval behind.

Valyn was a twisted swirl of guilt and helpless anger. Theren turned to face her.

"Val," he murmured.

"I'm sorry," she spat, turning away from him. He felt her try to hide her mind, but she wasn't particularly successful. "All I do is get you into trouble."

Theren took her knife and stowed both weapons again.

"What's life without a little trouble?" He smiled from the entrance to the hollow.

Valyn spun to face him. "Probably peaceful? I wouldn't know!"

Her anger shifted to something darker; shame, envy. Memories that didn't belong to him raced across Theren's mind, and he had to push Valyn out of his head.

"Can you stop that?" he chided. "Your thoughts are louder than a dracyr's roar." He cited the scaled, flightless birds that lurked in the darkest parts of the forest. Of course, Valyn had only ever seen one through Theren's memories, and he cringed at the error. Now was not the time to remind her of all she couldn't experience for herself.

She glared at him, and he smiled apologetically. He felt her anger waver, and he took her hand, guiding her to sit with him on the branch. She didn't resist. Theren leaned back on his hands and sighed as he watched the twinkling light from the spire below; like a mirror image of the night sky. The spire was beautiful, and he loved his people, but the roles of men and women had never quite fit Valyn.

"You're not leaving again until the Brother-walk?" Valyn asked, changing the subject.

"I doubt it. We can't leave until The Choosing, and then I doubt Hunt Master Feldan will take a band out before the Bro..."

Theren trailed off, realising his assumption. There was no guarantee Feldan would take him at The Choosing.

Valyn nudged him with her shoulder. "The Hunt really must have gone well, then," she teased.

"I'm sorry," Theren let his chagrin leak out between them.

"Don't be embarrassed. I have no doubt Feldan will choose you. You've always wanted this."

"Wanting something does not guarantee it," Theren murmured.

Valyn harrumphed, a grumble of anger and shame brewing in her again.

"As I well know," Valyn murmured. "Theren, why can't I be like everyone else?"

The injustice was clear to Theren; if he failed to join the Hunters it would be because he was assessed on merit and fell short. Valyn would never even get the chance to try.

"Have you ever considered that you aren't the problem?" Theren asked. "That maybe all this" — he gestured below — "needs to change? Not you."

The dismissing feeling from her suggested that she had not.

"Do *you* want it to change?" she asked. Theren felt her wash her thoughts away before he could read them in an unusual moment of self-control.

Theren nodded, their expressive communication the vestigial consequence of a shared childhood.

"Why?" she asked.

Why, indeed, when the current state of things advantaged him so? He could do everything she wished for herself: hunt, fight, adventure through the forest. He got to leave the spire on the Brotherwalk, and he had the suspicion it was not only the adventure of the journey that appealed to Valyn. She certainly thought of romance with more longing than he, whenever he'd caught her thinking about it.

"Just because you want the things I have, doesn't mean I want all of them," he found himself saying. Valyn's surprise jolted his mind. "Sorry," he mumbled, suddenly feeling foolish. "I should go. The Speaker won't leave me be if ignore Ylia's summons."

"Theren-"

Theren closed himself off, and all the confusion and shame within, some of it contagion from Valyn, disappeared. He squeezed his friend's hand once more and vaulted off the branch to return to the spire.

4

Theren's mother brushed Ylia's hair by the light of the warmheart. It was quiet, yet Theren could sense the tension caused by his presence. He knew his mother would have preferred him to have stayed at Roshin's that night.

"When will I get tested by the Dreamers?" he asked his mother, his curiosity getting the better of him. One of his classmates had not arrived at school that day, and the rumours were that they had been taken by the Dreamers in the night.

"I don't know," his mother replied.

"When did you get tested, Ylia?" Theren asked.

"Leave her alone, Theren!"

A memory emerged in Theren's mind of the Dreamer's Tower looming above him. Except it was Ylia's memory, not his.

It disappeared as Ial wrenched the brush through Ylia's hair with a fierce tug.

"Go to bed, Theren."

Theren stared at his sister, who refused to meet his eye.

Bed, Theren! *his mother bellowed in his mind.*

"But I want to know!"

Suddenly propelled by an unseen force, Theren walked himself from the room. He saw his mother's ithlyn flare brightly before he left. As quickly as it came over him, the feeling left, and he regained control of his body. He stared at his hands, all too familiar with the disorienting feeling of turning up in places he had no memory of travelling to.

He'd come to learn there was a word for it. Mind-walking; to take control of another person's consciousness and do with them what you will. Few were powerful enough to do it. None were allowed.

Yet here he was, standing in the corridor, despite having no desire to be there.

Though he rushed home after leaving Valyn, night had fallen by the time Theren saw his mother.

In typical fashion, she was unavailable when he first arrived at the Speaker's Tower, the highest building in the city and the seat of all power in Starspire. The grand hall on the first floor hosted exalted dignitaries from other spires on the rare occasions of their visits. On the floors above, the six members of the Speaker's Council met and argued their advice for their leader and guided the work of their subordinates in the six Professions. Speaker Ial's chambers were on the very top floors — interlinked rooms of glass archways and gossamer curtains ringed by an expansive balcony around the entire level. The structure was a monument to the Builders' prowess, gleaming brightly above the city to embody the authority of the Speaker's connection to Ena. The Speaker was the only one who spoke to their Entity, the only one who knew Ena's will. The privilege ran down the female line, each Speaker passing the role to their daughter. Traditionally, the Speaker only had one child, and she was always female. As Theren was often reminded, he had been a mistake.

Theren waited for his mother in her chambers, pacing the balcony. At that height, Ena's great trunk began to narrow and branch, like any tree would, forming a twisting ceiling of lesser branches and glinting leaves. Theren knew, higher above still, the dark canvas of the night sky would be twinkling with stars; stars he wished he could be watching now to soothe the knots in his stomach caused by his regret at his words to Valyn. He understood Valyn's angst better than anyone, possibly better than she did. Her constant dissatisfaction felt to him like she was caught in a tangle of vines, perpetually straining against the demands of society but never freeing herself. All she ever did was tighten the knots. It was disappointing because he, too, wouldn't mind if the vines were more relaxed, though he'd never admit it aloud. He pushed his shame away; at least Valyn was brave enough to be different. What did he do but comply with what was expected of him? He was an exemplary Speaker's son.

"Theren."

His mother's voice was as smooth as the glassy buildings of the spire and as cold as a cloudless night. She'd snuck up on him; no trace of her touching his mind. Theren echoed her obfuscation, tightening the barriers in his mind against any lapse that would reveal his inner world to her.

He turned from the web-like balustrade and offered her the formal Alvar greeting; touching his palm to his forehead then facing it toward her. *My mind is your mind,* the gesture said in place of words. There was irony in using such a greeting with her; it couldn't be farther from the truth.

The nights in Starspire were brighter than in the dark forests beyond, but even without the contrast of shadows, Speaker Ial was like a beacon. The light from the spire reflected off her pale skin, white gown, and silver hair — lending her an eerie glow. Like most of the women of Starspire, who never left the shelter of Ena's canopy, Ial's years could not be determined by lines on her face but rather by the wisdom in her pale blue eyes.

"You have returned from the Hunt," Ial stated the obvious. "How was it?"

She remained in the doorway to her chambers, framed by the translucent drapes that floated in an unnatural breeze. Theren remained at the edge of the balcony, nothing but empty air behind him.

"You are working late." Theren ignored her question. He knew she didn't care for the answer.

"I am always working," Ial stated with no hint of emotion. "Hunt Master Feldan tells me the Hunt was a success. No one lost."

"Only some minor injuries," Theren confirmed. What was this? She didn't need him to report on the Hunt.

Ial took a few steps towards him, her gown swishing around her long legs. Despite the reduced distance between them, a chasm remained.

"You will be leaving soon."

"The Brotherwalk," Theren acknowledged, hoping the twinge of trepidation he felt at the affair was hidden from her.

"Yes, the Brotherwalk."

The sounds of night creatures hummed softly around them.

"There is The Choosing first, of course." Ial took a few steps closer.

"And Ena's light is blue," Theren snapped. "Is this just a conversation of stating the obvious?" He let a shot of impatience out from behind his barrier. With that foolish action, his mask slipped, and his mother got a chance to gain purchase in his mind.

"Ah. You were with Valyn. That's why you didn't come straight to me." The impression of Valyn's face swam behind his eyes along with a feeling of resounding disappointment. "She has always been a bad influence on you."

Theren tried to quiet his mind, pressing his emotions deep into the mental chasm he'd long ago cultivated in defence of his privacy. Ial shook her head at him, just like she had done when he was a child.

"I make my own choices." Theren glared at her. "You can't place the blame at her feet every time I do something you don't like."

Ial strode towards him, the pretence at civility dropped now that she'd won.

"I can do whatever I like," she levelled at him, her gaze cold. "If it wasn't for her, there wouldn't be that dissatisfaction I sense brewing in you."

Though he wished to glare at her, to send forth a wave of anger, he restrained himself. Such actions required him to feel something, and she would use that to get inside his mind again.

Ial held his gaze, and he could feel her trying to search him. She leaned closer, and though he was grown now and taller than she, he somehow felt like he was a small boy once more. Her face inches from him, she let a smile tug at the corner of her mouth.

"Your mind is strong. I've raised you well."

Theren didn't flinch at her proximity, forcing himself to not to exhibit any feeling.

"You had little role in raising me," he retorted, carefully controlling the twinge of disdain he sent out with the barb.

Before Ial could answer, he sensed Ylia's mind brushing over them both. Ial straightened. Ylia needed Theren's help with the baby.

Theren was probably the only boy who would feel relieved to be called upon to help care for an infant, usually the job of children and women. Once he had completed his Brotherwalk, his sister would never again ask him for assistance with such a thing.

"Good night, Speaker."

He didn't look back as he hurried to his sister, who would never realise the extent to which she had unwittingly saved him.

"Of course, I realised." Ylia scrunched her face at him as though he was little older than the toddler that he now bounced on his knee. "I didn't actually need help with Elska."

Theren held his niece gently under her arms as he jiggled her up and down on his leg. Her little giggles of joy forced a smile to his face despite himself. Safe within the confines of Ylia's rooms in the Speaker's Tower, the tension of his encounter with their mother slowly melted away. He leaned back in the soft cushions and fabric that covered the glass, bowl-like chairs arranged around the warmheart; a warm, glowing orb commonly found floating in the middle of every home in Starspire that provided warmth and light.

"So why did you call me?" Theren asked.

Ylia scoffed and returned to the kitchenette. Never mind how old the two of them were, Ylia had never seemed to shake the expressive habits of childhood when she was with him.

"You were about to throw yourself off that balcony if you had to stay with Mother a second longer." Ylia spoke in his mind.

Theren shared his trepidation with her. "I thought I'd hidden myself."

She sent back her impression of his face locked in a sinister stare, realising it was from their mother's perspective. Ylia had not witnessed the interaction through him, but rather through their mother's eyes.

He shook his head in disbelief. To observe their interactions through Ial's eyes, without Ial noticing? If Ial thought she was powerful, Ylia was truly something else. Fitting, then, that she would be the next Speaker of Starspire. Hopefully, she would be kinder than their current one.

"Your mind may be hard to find, but I have my ways of watching you," Ylia replied aloud, sending out a playful current of exaggerated drama as she returned from the kitchen with an urn of warm tisane and a plate of dried fruits. While Ena provided food in abundance through the arts of the Growers, anything sun-dried was considered a delicacy for the effort it took to reach the upper canopy and face the open air and sunshine. Never mind that the Growers could use their Light to dry things in an instant with little difference in the taste.

Little Elska leaned recklessly forward to grab at the plate, and Theren saved her from tumbling off his leg, turning her to face him.

"Not for you Elsie." He smiled broadly at her. She mirrored his grin; mischief personified. He felt a flicker of maternal pride and familial warmth from Ylia, and he glanced towards where she sat in the opaque glass chair across from him. She watched him with a soft smile, her silvery hair crushed where she rested her hand on her cheek, the shadow of a smile playing on her lips.

"You're a good uncle, Ren."

Theren's fondness was tinged with sadness. Once he was considered a man, it would be unseemly for Ylia to include him in raising Elska like this. If they had a sister, the duty would remain with her. As it was, Ylia relied on friends and other mothers within their echelon to care for Elska on the days she was occupied by the business of learning to be Speaker. Much of Elska's early years would be shaped by the parenting of other mothers until her own journey to become Speaker began.

"I'll make sure I teach her to spoil you." Ylia's eyes sparkled as she caught his thoughts, handing Theren his warm drink.

Theren kept the thick, glass mug away from Elska's hands and pulled her in close for a cuddle. Her protests quickly quieted as she snuggled into his chest.

"You'll be a good Speaker, Elsie," he murmured into her pale curls. He looked up at his sister. "You will be, too."

Ylia held his gaze as she sipped her steaming drink.

"I'll try, Ren. I'll try."

5

Theren sat on a high branch at the edge of the forest, gazing out across the silver fields of the open valley at night. Ena's glow thrummed behind him, veins of Light illuminating the trees and the leaves around him. The life of the spire was like the trickle of a distant stream, and though he felt it all, he held himself apart. He did not want to be discovered on this illicit trip to the edge of the forest. No one was supposed to leave the spire, save the Hunters or the Speaker herself, especially not children.

But how could he resist? His eyes wandered over the broken spire in the valley below, wondering, imagining. What were the Void like? What happened to their tower? Had it collapsed that fateful day when the Alvar finally defeated them? What were those days like? Only the Listeners knew, and they guarded the past like a dracys guarded its nest.

A sparkle in the corner of his eye caught Theren's attention. It glinted within the waving branches. Theren froze, realising the folly of this excursion. No creature connected to Ena's Light would attack him, but a Light-mad beast or a wandering animal from the outer forest would.

He remained frozen for long minutes, watching the shimmer blink in and out of view. He realised it was something obscured behind the leaves — not a creature after all. His courage renewed, he leapt to the source hiding among the branches below.

Facing into the open valley was a sigil carved into the tree trunk, crafted from the same pale blue Light of Starspire. Theren rested his hand upon it. It was warm under his palm, but it didn't react with purpose like a sigil in the spire. Indeed, nothing happened at all. Theren had never thought much about the sigils, in the same way he didn't think much about Light — it simply was — but for the first time he was curious. What was a sigil doing out here?

Clinging to the tree, he turned and looked out over the valley; the broken spire a hulking shadow in the night. Perhaps the sigil had no reason to do anything, anymore.

Theren awoke the next morning to a heavy weight on his chest and a barrage of giggles in his face.

"Elsie!" Theren laughed as he pushed her off into his soft mattress and a swathe of blanket. Elsie's giggles persisted beside him, and he felt Ylia's mirth from the doorway of his room.

"You slept late," his sister said as she came over to retrieve the wriggling bundle of energy she had clearly set on him only moments before. It was one of her favourite ways of waking him up; a game she and Elska delighted in, testing how long the little one could stay silent beside her uncle before she inevitably broke out in laughter.

Theren felt a pang of loss, premature, but no less real. As he was still a child in the eyes of the spire, he got away with living with Ylia. It was acceptable for a boy to remain with his family until he came of age, and after much supplication to their mother, Ial had allowed Theren to reside within Ylia's chambers rather than higher up in the rooms adjacent to hers.

It was yet another reason Theren regarded the Brotherwalk with some trepidation. Despite Ylia's bossy nature and the additional work of child-rearing, it was far nicer arriving home to soft hugs from small arms and a reasonable voice with sound advice than to live alone. He was not eager to return to an empty dwelling with only his own thoughts for company.

"What's wrong?" Ylia asked, and Theren shut off his mind. Ylia was too good at reading him.

"Nothing."

Ylia frowned, her eyes inspecting his face.

"Sleep poorly?"

"No, why?"

"You look tired."

Theren stood up and threw his hand behind him, sending out his Light to order the blankets into arranging themselves. They flew up in a flurry before settling neatly on the bed.

"Lazy," Ylia scoffed.

Theren flashed her a childish grin, amplifying his disagreement towards her. It took a lot of finesse and skill to manipulate an object into moving.

"What do you want for breakfast?" Theren asked before Ylia could scold him again. She was a stickler for appreciating manual labour; those who did not have Ylia's and Theren's strength with their Light, which was most people, would have found it easier to make the bed by hand.

"I have an early meeting with the Speaker's Council," she explained, adjusting Elska on her hip, who was imitating Theren's wave at the blankets. "Can you watch Elsie for a few hours?"

"Ren! Ren!" Elska cried, reaching for her uncle. Theren bowed to her and held his hand out in front of him, conjuring a ball of silver-blue light, which exploded into an array of tiny shimmers that he sent towards the little girl. She shrieked with delight.

"I'll take that as a yes," Ylia said, handing her daughter over with a flicker of wry judgement.

"How long will you be?" Theren asked, lifting Elska up onto his shoulders. She reached for the little stars he sent up to dance around her face.

"A few hours. I will let you know when I return."

"It won't be long until you have to find someone else to do this for you, Ylia," Theren warned, softening the words with his regret.

"Maybe I'll ask Valyn," Ylia teased as she turned to leave. "That'll serve as just punishment for yesterday."

Theren chuckled to himself and patted Elsie's leg.

"Auntie Valyn is a lot of wonderful things," Theren said to Elska. "But good with children is not one of them."

Theren fixed Elska some breakfast, allowing her to sit on his shoulders for the duration of the preparation. The little amulet tied around her bare ankle prevented any mind-linking or sharing of emotions until he reached up to cover it with his hand and pushed past its block.

The purest pleasure emanated from her, intermingled with anticipation for the food she could smell and a warm, deep affection for the uncle upon whose shoulders she felt so safe. Theren removed his hand, his chest fluttering. The mind of a young child was intense; thoughts that didn't quite make sense and feelings that were overpoweringly pure.

"Thank Ena we don't remember any of that when we grow up," Theren mumbled to himself, heating in his hands the cup of redfruit tisane he'd prepared. Turning his mind to the day ahead, he played over his conversation with Valyn yesterday. He should have stood up for her against his friends, he thought with regret, and he should not have chided her like he was her parent.

"Elsie," he said to the toddler as he took her to the sitting room, placing her on the floor beside the warmheart for her to eat her breakfast. "Uncle Theren was mean to Auntie Valyn yesterday..."

Elska picked up a piece of fruit and shook her head at him. "Bad, Ren."

"Exactly. What do we do when we've done something wrong?"

"Say sorry."

After they both finished eating, he set about getting himself and Elska dressed for the day. The chores of organising a small child occupied his mind fully, and it wasn't until Elska insisted on trying to put on her own shoes that he finally had a chance to cast his mind out across Starspire to find Valyn.

The collective minds of the city could be likened to a group of people all simultaneously singing their own song. One may focus on one voice alone and hear all the words and melody of their singing. Conversely, one can hear the whole chorus and make very little sense of anything. Or one could tune them all out and get on with what they were doing. There is also the fact of your own singing; one must learn to moderate one's volume as needed. The mind cannot be turned off, but its volume is measured by the impact it has on others. As anyone who has spent any time around children knows, they are harder to ignore, hence the amulets that neutralised their Light. It allowed children the time to mature before they joined the collective link of the spire.

It was not hard to find Valyn. Not that she was loud, although she could be, but her mind was so familiar to him that he was drawn to it easily. She was trying to quieten her thoughts, which were rippling with anticipation, as she made her way through the lower echelons of the spire.

"All done!" Elska proudly announced, standing before him with her shoes on the wrong feet. Theren refocused on the little girl in front of him and shook his head.

Valyn would have to wait a little longer.

When he finally caught up to Valyn, Elska's shoes were still on the wrong feet and Valyn's thoughts had shifted from anticipation to wonder.

Theren stood in front of the Weavers' workshop; a huge dome on a rise caused by one of Ena's roots that displaced the very earth through which it grew. Two tall, opaque glass doors — easily the height of four people — guarded the entrance, a sigil engraved across both that would open them with a mere touch. Inside, all Starspire's fabrications were made; curtains, clothing, rugs, rope, blankets — anything that couldn't be conjured by the power of Light or made by the Builders. Few citizens had business directly in the workshop, and Theren doubted Valyn was there on business.

What are you doing in there? Theren thought to his friend as he approached the entrance.

A shimmer of guilt, overlaid with a vision of the ogyr he had helped bring home from the Hunt, told him all he needed to know. He didn't have to know the specifics to know she was doing something she really wasn't supposed to.

I was hoping to increase my chances of being selected by a Profession, she replied. *By doing some research.*

It was a lie, and not a very good one. While it was true that Valyn needed all the help she could get to be chosen by a Profession at The

Choosing in two days' time, it was unlike her to ever do anything that would help herself. Besides, she had shown no aptitude for Weaving. She would be better off ingratiating herself with the Listeners; they were the Profession with which she had shown the most talent and interest. Then again, the historians of the spire would no doubt be reluctant to have someone like Valyn taint the records of history with her contrarian views.

Theren sighed and tapped Elsie's leg as he pointed to the huge doors of the workshop.

"Ready Elsie?"

Elska roared and flung her hand out before her as though she were single-handedly slaughtering an ogyr. As she did so, Theren pushed the huge doors of the workshop open with a flare of his Light, the heavy glass gliding inwards with no sign of the mental effort it took to move them.

He felt Valyn's disdain.

You could've opened the door like everyone else, you know.

And waste the element of surprise?

Show off.

Theren walked into the workshop, past the sigil on the now-open doors. The sigils of Starspire were not overly common; those living within Ena's purview were interconnected by her Light and thus easily manipulated the world around them. However, not all citizens were as strong with their power as others, and for tasks that required great exertion, or where two people may have conflicting desires, it was easier to rely on the sigils. It was the only form of written communication the Alvar used; each imbued with a specific magical command that would be enacted upon contact with a citizen's Light, no matter how weak their skill.

In addition to the common sigils, each Profession also had their own set that assisted their craft. By far the Builders were the masters of written Light. There were a lot of things to consider when crafting the very city under their feet.

"Speakerson!" called a nearby supervisor as Theren strode into the huge, open hall. He bowed towards Theren, pressing his palm against his forehead then turning it outwards. It was overly formal for the context, but Theren was the son of the Speaker, and that demanded every demonstration of respect available.

Theren returned the greeting with a hint of reassurance emanating toward the man, watching the Weaver's eyes wander up to Elska sitting on his shoulders. Though largely hidden beneath the supervisor's uncertainty, Theren felt his judgement. It was unseemly for a man to be seen carrying a child like that, and Theren was close enough in age to be considered as such.

"I bring with me the future Speaker herself, Weaver...?"

Theren could have taken the man's name from his mind if he wanted but he wasn't in the business of stealing people's thoughts.

"Weaver Mithel." The man bowed again, once more glancing up at Elska. "And welcome to you, too, err, Apprentice-Speakers-Daughter."

"Say hello, Elska," Theren directed his niece while scanning the expanse of the factory floor. He couldn't see Valyn but he sensed her in the lower rooms to the rear of the workshop. No doubt that was where they were storing the ogyr while they prepared it for use.

What do you want? Valyn flicked her irritation at him.

"I came to find Valyn Roshinsdaughter," Theren explained to the Weaver, who blanched at the mention of her name.

"We insisted she shouldn't be here, Speakerson," the Weaver said, his regret and placation rolling off him in waves. "She is not a Weaver, nor a Hunter, and has no need to see it."

Valyn's familiar head appeared at the back of the workshop from over a sea of looms and worktables strewn with all manner of inventions.

"Nothing is wrong, good Weaver. We're needed elsewhere, and I've come to collect her." Theren once again reassured the nervous man.

Theren stepped aside to watch Valyn approach. She wore slim-fitting leggings and an overly large shirt in hues of soft mauve, which complemented her pale complexion nicely. Much to her mother's disappointment, Valyn was rarely seen in a dress.

"Hello Elska." Valyn waved at Theren's niece. Elska waved back.

What's she doing here?

I'm on babysitting duty for a few hours.

Valyn didn't need words to tell Theren what she thought of *that*.

"Thank you, Weaver Mithel," Valyn sent her appreciation out to the Weaver, guiding Theren outside. Like Theren, she pushed the doors closed behind her with the use of her Light, though she expended more energy than he did with the action, causing her ithlyn to flare brightly for a moment.

"You scolded me for doing that only moments ago!" Theren objected.

Valyn grinned at him, her flippant pleasure like warm sunshine. "I know."

Her mood shifted from one of mischief to awe, and Theren saw in his mind's eye what she had just seen in the Weaver's storeroom; the ogyr stretched out over a thick glass slab, flakes of ice creeping up over the corpse to prevent decay.

"So can we expect your name to be called by the Head Weaver in a couple of days?" Theren teased, reminding her of her poor excuse.

Valyn wrinkled her nose at him.

"Fine, I lied. I just wanted to see it. It's so huge! I can't believe you killed it..." Theren pushed down his regret at the deed. "It got me thinking, especially when you ignored the sigil on the door before," Valyn continued, her words stumbling over themselves. "The sigils are used without most people even thinking about them.

But they could have so much more value. We could protect the spire from creatures like the ogyr, for example."

"But are creatures even impacted by sigils?" Theren wondered, as they walked up the steps, away from the workshop. "How would we-"

A rush of Valyn's ideas buffeted him; half-formed and tinged with excitement, formulating something around designing new sigils for rebuffing creatures from their surrounds. The ogyr was the target of her first half-cocked experiment.

"I don't know yet," she said aloud. "But it's an interesting question, don't you think?"

Theren sent her a wave of fondness.

"If you think so, then I think so."

"Ugh. Don't patronise me."

"Don't batanise me!" echoed Elska from above. Valyn laughed.

"Great." Theren sighed. "I'll have to explain that to Ylia."

"Just don't tell her it was my fault," Valyn snorted, though a hint of genuine concern lay beneath the words. They continued across a bridge arching over a small gully, lush, dark foliage beneath them. From here, Theren could see the soft glow of Ena's springs below, tucked between enormous roots and hidden safely in the heart of the spire.

"Anyway, where are we going?" Valyn asked. "What do you want?"

The answer to that caused him to hesitate. Though the excuse to come find her was the apology he owed, he truly had come to find her out of habit — a habit that would be curtailed in just a few short days. He hid the familiar pang of uncertainty. It was a great honour to be called upon for a Hunter's apprenticeship, and it wasn't gloating to assume that's where he was headed, but it would mean far less time spent in the spire. Not to mention, he'd be gone on the Brotherwalk soon. This might be one of their last few days together for a long time. Their final days of childhood felt like they were slipping through his fingers.

He felt a shift of energy beside him and saw Valyn's ithlyn flare slightly as she attempted to eavesdrop on his mind.

"Hey!" He pulled his thoughts back.

"I wouldn't have to push if you weren't invisible half the time!"

"I'm not!"

"You are," she argued. "You're like a shadow — little more than an empty space where a person is supposed to be." She waved her hands at him accusingly.

Theren knew he was good at hiding his mind but was surprised to hear that Valyn struggled to hear him too. Their bond was so strong, he assumed she could still feel his presence at least.

"Why don't we go see your mother?" Theren suggested, both attempting to change the subject and to avoid her original question.

"As long as you don't tell her where you found me," Valyn acquiesced. While seeing Roshin was a good diversion, Theren also genuinely wanted to see her. He could do with some sage words and a distraction, and though Valyn was excellent at providing the latter, the former was not her strength.

6

Theren sat by the warmheart in Roshin's home, weary after training all day with the Hunters. He had done well for himself, earning much approval from Hunt Master Feldan.

"What was that, love?" Roshin's voice called from the kitchen.

"I didn't say anything," Theren replied. Valyn was not home yet, though he didn't know where she was. She still wore her amulet for much of the day, shamefully old to be still doing so, and thus was impossible to find.

Roshin came into the room, a tea towel draped over her shoulder.

"You're very quiet."

"I don't want to talk to you while you're busy," Theren replied, sending out deference.

Roshin sighed, easing herself down beside him.

"I don't mean quiet like that. I mean, I can barely feel you, even though you're only a few feet away."

Theren simply shrugged.

Why do you dampen your thoughts so? *she asked in his mind.*

"I don't," he replied aloud. He was familiar with this trick; she was trying to get a read on him.

"It must take a lot of energy," she replied, this time aloud. "You hold back so tightly I wonder if you can even relax while you sleep."

He felt a twinge of frustration. He wasn't trying to do anything.

Roshin put an arm around him and pulled him tight against her.

"One day, you won't need to keep people out," she murmured into his hair, the feeling emanating from her fierce and warm. Theren's mind wavered...if only he could tell her. He would tell her how much he wished she was his mother, how he wished he never had to go back to the Speaker's Tower.

But Theren knew better than to open a box you weren't sure you could close again.

Theren and Valyn made their way up through the city, the soft light of the spire casting a cool glow around them. Theren talked nonsense with Elska, keeping her distracted and entertained on his shoulders. He caught Valyn inspecting him from the corner of her eye, the tendrils of her mind brushing against his. He tightened his thoughts, though he hadn't been thinking of much. It was an instinct honed over years.

"What was it like?" Valyn asked aloud. "Killing it?"

The image of the ogyr lying dead on the table in the Weaver's storeroom swam behind his eyes while Valyn's awe reverberated in his chest.

"A grim question," Theren replied, lifting his arms to grab Elska's hands from poking his face. He gathered his thoughts. "Killing anything is hard," he replied. "Even if it's attacking you."

"But you had to kill it, for the safety of the spire."

"I know, but that doesn't make it any easier."

He felt a hint of exasperation from her but he didn't share his own irritation. She didn't know what it was like. All she could think about was how she wished she could know. He changed the subject before she could argue with him.

"Your idea about the sigils, about using them for protection... I've seen one that might be exactly what you're talking about."

He finally got Elska to stop poking at his eyes by giving her a flower he had plucked from a nearby vine, imbuing the pistil with a small light.

"You have?"

Theren shared a memory with her of the sigil carved into the trunk of the tree he had seen outside the spire.

"Where is it?"

"At the edge of the forest," he explained.

"Which edge?"

"The edge-edge," he replied, accompanying the answer with an image of the trees opening into the fields of the Abyss beyond, devoid of forest and exposed to the elements. Ena's forest radiated in a circle around the Starspire until it was eventually surrounded, in turn, by a regular forest, which connected all Alvaren. The only exception to that design was a small section where Ena's forest met the Abyss.

"What's a sigil doing out there?" she asked.

"I don't know," Theren replied. "I don't think anyone knows about it. I thought it might have something to do with the Void."

At the mention of the Void, Valyn's excitement flared from where she walked beside him; he could almost feel it as a wash of heat against his arm. Valyn truly would be most at home with the Listeners. Aside from wanting to run through the forest with the Hunters, she had always been hungry for knowledge and puzzles. He held out hope the Listeners would see all that she had to offer at The Choosing.

"How can no one know about it?" Valyn scoffed.

Theren gave her a mental shrug. "It doesn't seem to do anything." He caught her thought before she'd even fully formed it. "Fine, I'll show you one day."

She grinned at him as she sent him her satisfaction.

"You're a good friend."

More like a fool, he replied in her mind.

They wound their way along a final turn of the walkway, arriving at Valyn's humble home; an opaque sphere of crystal under a forest of flowering and fruiting vines.

Theren felt a greeting pass between Valyn and her mother. Moments later, Roshin bustled out the front door, dressed in a simple, blue dress with a white apron overlaid. Theren was buffeted with a wind of pride and warmth.

"Speakerson," Roshin said, face impassive. As soon as they were inside, the door closed behind them, Roshin's round face lit up in delight. "And you've brought the Apprentice-Apprentice Speaker herself!"

She waved to Elska. Elska returned the gesture with enthusiasm, and Theren caught a glimmer of Roshin's memories of Valyn doing a similar thing when she was younger. He extricated his niece from his shoulders, and as soon as the little girl was on the ground, Roshin bundled Theren up in an enthusiastic embrace. Her head rested against his chest, and he found himself missing the days where the positions were reversed.

"You're taller," Roshin accused. "Every time I see you, you look older."

"Roshin, you see me at least once a week," he laughed.

"And that's still not nearly enough." Roshin's face creased in a dramatic frown, as if he was still five years old and she was chasing him in a game of monsters. He felt his heart swell and looked to his feet as he tried to crush the feeling. After his mother's grip in his mind the prior night, he was conscious of keeping his mental vice tight — any strong emotion might jeopardise that.

"Valyn," Roshin turned to where Valyn was playing with Elska. A request passed between them faster than Theren could discern.

"Ugh, fine," Valyn replied, and she trudged off with Elska to her bedroom. "Come on, Elsie. Let me show you my old toys."

"You're very quiet," Roshin said to Theren as he followed her to the kitchen. "I can't even tell if you're hungry."

"I'm talking to you, aren't I?" Theren smiled, resting his hip on the edge of the kitchen table. "Besides, I'm always hungry."

"That's not what I meant and you know it," Roshin replied with a gentle rebuke. "And don't lean on the table."

Theren jumped up while she bustled around the kitchen. His attempts to help were met with a forceful mental shove so he simply sat down — on a chair this time — and watched.

Roshin Freyasdaughter was born to be a mother. Her long, opalescent hair was swept up in a loose bun, a scarf holding it in place to protect it from the labours of her day. She hummed a tune as she tossed some green vegetables, which she had no doubt picked from her little garden that morning; the garden that grew over the top of her round, glass home, obscuring the view from the windows and causing heads to turn whenever they walked past. Roshin would have been chosen by the Growers, no doubt, if Ial hadn't asked her to be her aide in their youth. Though he didn't know the details, he sensed Roshin and Ial's friendship had waned over the years. Roshin still served in the Speaker's Tower, but Ial had found others to wait on her directly these days.

"Isn't it lonely?" Roshin asked. "Being disconnected from everyone?"

"I'm not disconnected," Theren replied, slouching into the chair. "I feel everyone."

Roshin set the urn down on the glass table and pulled a chair forward to sit knee-to-knee with him. She rested her hand on his leg.

"Connection is a two-way road, love. To really be close to someone, you have to let them feel you too."

Theren reached for Valyn, who was only just tolerating Elska's ransacking of her old toys. He felt Valyn's acknowledgement.

"Mother!" Valyn shouted from the bedroom. "Where did we put my old chest of dresses?"

Roshin sighed lengthily before patting Theren on the leg and leaving the kitchen.

Thanks, he whispered in Valyn's mind.

Roshin meant well, and he owed everything to her for the happiness she had brought him over the years. But her warnings were futile; some habits were so ingrained he wasn't sure he knew how to break them.

7

Theren gaped, not caring that the action revealed his immaturity in front of the Hunters.

A thrum of mirth ran through him from the men.

"It's something, isn't it?"

Theren simply nodded. The edge of the forest was abrupt — one moment there were trees, the next there was empty air. Only rolling fields and open sky beyond.

"What's that?" Theren pointed at a ruin in the meadows, cracked in half like a small spire had been toppled.

"No one knows," one of the Hunters replied. "It could be an old Alvar spire or it could have belonged to the Void."

Mirth turned to disturbance as everyone considered their ancient enemy; a long-extinct race that had tried to destroy them a thousand years ago. Theren's heart *skipped with worry but he knew the feeling did not belong solely to him. All the Alvar felt an ancient fear at the mention of the Void.*

Strangely, though he took care to hide it, beside the fear, Theren also felt wonder.

Later that night, when he and Valyn lay in her bed, another night spent in Roshin's home, he told her about it; the broken spire and the edge of the forest. With his hand wrapped around her amulet, he felt her excitement as she begged him to show her. He could not deny her.

Besides, he wanted someone to talk to about it; someone as fearless as him. Someone who understood the call to adventure, the thrill of the old tales.

Everything was better when he could share it with Valyn.

With Elska finally asleep, Theren collapsed on his bed in his room in Ylia's apartment. He loved his niece more than just about anything, but, by Ena, he was glad he didn't have to be a mother full-time. No wonder the women of Starspire shared the load of child rearing collectively. From his bed, which was curved at the head to fit the circular room, he was able to watch the open doorway, where he kept expecting to see

Elska appear, begging him to come back and tell one more story.

He didn't know how late Ylia would be but he didn't bother her with the question. Learning to be the Speaker was surely the most taxing job in the spire, and its responsibilities kept her back many a night. It was the same reason he had spent so many nights of his childhood in Roshin's care, as Ial first shadowed her mother and then took over leadership of the spire when her time came. Though Roshin's home was smaller, humbler, and he had to share a room with Valyn when he stayed over, it was a far better place to rest one's head than within the cold opulence of the Speaker's quarters.

Theren gazed around his room, which was larger than Roshin's kitchen and living area combined. Swathes of diaphanous fabric hung around his bed, suspended from the domed roof. The ceiling was imbued with an image of a clear night sky, a touch Theren himself had placed that proved he would be just as welcome among the Builders as the Hunters. The warmheart in the centre of the room hovered just above its spindle-like podium, emitting a pale blue light. Theren waved his hand, Ena's power shifting within him, and dimmed the light slightly. The warmth that emanated from it remained as he sat up on the bed and untied the laces of his vest. His body still ached from the days on the Hunt and a full day of running around after his niece.

Though a warm bath in his private washroom was appealing, Theren took off his outer layer of clothing and lay back down on the bed, wrapping the covers around himself. His mind wandered to The Choosing and the Brotherwalk. But, mostly, he kept thinking about everything he was about to lose. With a melancholy sigh, he realised that today had been his last proper chance to enjoy his niece's company, and potentially Valyn's too. With the duties of adulthood about to call, their mischievous adventures were over.

He reached out for Valyn and her familiar presence was with him almost instantly. She was trying to sleep but she was not content. When was she ever? With a smile, he rolled over, pulling his soft blankets up around his chin.

Good night, Val, he murmured in her mind, sending her an impression of a starry sky from a memory they'd shared many years ago.

Are you snooping on me? Valyn shot back gently.

Someone has to look out for you. She sent her dismissal in a mental scoff, but Theren could feel the warmth beneath it. *I never told you why I came to find you today,* he continued.

To rope me in to helping you take care of Elska?

I think that would get me in trouble for endangering a child.

Ha, ha. Why then?

He recalled the memory of their argument the day before, allowing himself to share his regret for his harsh words.

Your words weren't harsh, Valyn reassured him.

They were uncalled for.

No, you were right. About my anger, about everything. Val...

I wish I was different, Theren, but I don't know how to be anything other than what I am.

Valyn had always been unique. Better, in Theren's mind. She was honest, and fun, and saw beyond the rigid rules of the spire. He hoped the Listeners would take her, for her perspective on Alvar culture could potentially influence things for the better. Unfortunately, few seemed to share his view of her value.

I'm not sure what's harder: changing yourself or changing the world, he replied.

Valyn agreed. A memory drifted between them, so closely connected neither was sure who thought it first; two children with their hands intertwined, falling asleep with their amulets touching.

Will you fall asleep with me?

Theren barely formed the request in words, and Valyn's reply was little more than a feeling.

Theren's sadness and Valyn's angst settled in moments, replaced by a familiar calm that welcomed sleep's embrace.

8

Theren stumbled into his mother's room, still fighting the haze of sleep. She was awake, wrapped in a warm gown over her nightdress and moving to the door towards him. She must have heard his mental calls to her.

"What is it?"

Her spear of concern shot through him, intermingling with his own fear and panic.

Theren rubbed his eyes, trying to stop the tears.

"I had a bad dream," he stammered. "You can't go on the Speakerswalk."

Ial put her hands firmly on his shoulders and shook him slightly. It jolted him awake, his mind clearing and his eyes better able to open.

"What's wrong with Theren?" Ylia's voice came from behind him.

"Go back to bed, Ylia."

"What's wrong?"

Theren cowered as he felt the thunderous fury directed at Ylia from their mother. He felt Ylia leave, not another word spoken.

Ial crouched down and smoothed Theren's hair back.

"It was just a dream, Theren. Nothing to worry about."

Theren shook his head.

"It was real."

"Dreams aren't real," Ial replied.

"But, Mother..." Theren pressed on, unable to fight the urge to tell her. To warn her. "In this dream, you died..."

Theren and Valyn slept as one.

While the minds of Starspire were interconnected by Ena's light, each citizen maintained their individual selves apart from the others. With time, infants grew to have their own sense of self, which was why it was so important they wear the amulets from the moment they were born. No one knew the psychological impact of being interconnected from birth. However, that sense of separation could be erased if a stronger person overtook the mind of a weaker one, or if both people consented and joined consciousness.

In the soft glow of night, Theren was both himself and Valyn, sharing her experience of the unconscious world as she shared his. Asleep, he made no sense of it; the glimpses of memory and loose thoughts, a longing for something, no — *someone* — forbidden, a grief for something not yet lost.

A heavy, panicked feeling pressed down on his body, as though someone was pushing him, pressing against him relentlessly, and he gasped, lurching awake in his bed. The light from the warmheart had gone out, and only the dim, pale blue glow from the walls illuminated the room. Breathing heavily, he gripped the covers and realised he was wearing his gloves. Hadn't he taken those off before bed?

He pushed back the covers and raised his hand to the dark warmheart as he stood, but the light did not return. Looking down in the gloom, he realised he was wearing armour.

The room swirled suddenly, as though reality was being sucked away. Theren's stomach lurched like he was falling and he stumbled.

The scene reorganised itself. He was not in his room anymore.

He stood on the forest floor. It was dark. Normally the Alvar moved through the forests from the safety of the interconnected branches, only coming down to the forest floor when they needed to cross a clearing, or when the trees thinned in the lesser forests beyond the protection of their Entity. Though Theren was familiar with the forest surrounding Starspire, he couldn't discern his location from the ground. The familiar bluish hue seeping from the trees around him reassured him that he was still within Ena's purview.

Something nudged his mind, just a hint, and he somehow knew it to be far away. He felt a pull ahead of him and he stumbled forward, unable to resist the urge to move towards it. He ran through the forest, trees and vines giving way to his careening path as though he were running through a crowd. The darkness loomed ahead, a curtain of light beyond. It was then he realised where he was.

He was at the edge of the forest; except, instead of looking out over open fields, he was staring out into a white curtain of nothing.

A gnawing feeling pressed against his mind, like he was fighting off someone trying to spy on him. Panic flared within him; what if it was Ial? He tried to quiet his mind, to hold his thoughts close to his chest, but he felt unravelled, untethered.

Memories of his time at the edge of the forest raced through his mind — first with the Hunters as a boy, then when he discovered the symbol at the forest edge. Not all the memories were his, though. He watched himself through Valyn's eyes as he excitedly leapt from tree to tree. Ena, they were so young!

He shook his head and tried to focus, but the white abyss before him expanded, seeping into his vision, enveloping him until he was surrounded by emptiness. He could not tell whether he was standing, lying, sitting, or floating.

All he saw was the familiar symbol of a sigil floating before his eyes, glowing with Ena's silver-blue light. The pressure around him built until he felt as if he were being squeezed. Panic rose in his throat, and the symbol flashed so brightly he had to close his eyes. Still, he could see it, almost burnt into his eyelids.

He reached out to touch it, and then there was nothing.

Theren awoke with no fanfare, no lurching gasp or kick of the covers, but his heart raced nonetheless. The instant he realised he was awake, he pulled his mind shut and held his face into his pillow, breathing heavily. He didn't feel anyone trying to get in. Hopefully he was safe.

Looking around the room, everything appeared normal. The warmheart was glowing softly, lighting the room. His clothes were on the floor where he'd dropped them; the stars of his ceiling twinkled innocently as though nothing had happened.

But something *had* happened. Theren could still feel it. The tug in his chest urged him towards the edge of the forest; the pressure in his mind felt as though someone was nudging against it, probing and prodding, trying to get in. It had felt so real, standing at the edge of the Abyss, though of course, it could not have been. Were he truly to stand at that place in the forest, he would have seen the rolling hills of the open landscape, glistening monochrome in the night.

The thought gave him an idea.

He threw back the covers and helped them to fall back on his bed neatly with a flick of his Light.

He was going to see for himself what in Ena's name was going on.

Erring on the side of caution, he put on as much of his armour as he could manage alone, swapping the full cuirass with a more flexible leather vest, as well as his good boots and gloves. His bow and quiver he slung across his back; his knife he tucked against his thigh.

Ensuring he kept his mind quiet, he stole from his window and onto the smooth glass roof of the room below. Starspire glowed beneath him, darkness never completely falling around the great city. Within minutes of careful climbing and leaping — some jumps assisted with a flare of his Light — he was gone from the spire and high in Ena's branches.

"Please just let this be a strange dream and nothing else," he whispered to the tree, resting his hand on its ancient bark before leaping out into the forest.

The levels of the canopy varied, like strata of rock. The highest branches were slim and flexible, waving with disturbance with the wind from the world outside the forest.

The mid-levels were a tangle of branches, vines, leaves, and nesting animals all interweaving in an ordered chaos that required skill to traverse but which was, by far, the fastest route. The branches were thick enough to run across with confidence, but when you needed it, a vine or slimmer branch would always be available to slingshot your journey from one tree to the next.

The lowest branches were broad and sturdy, the reliable roads of the forest. They did not always intersect at convenient points, though, meaning one could travel with little fear of falling but with limited efficiency.

The forest floor, of course, was neither safe nor efficient, and thus was typically avoided unless one was on the Hunt.

Theren chose the familiar twists of the middle part of the forest; weaving, winding, leaping, and climbing through the cool air of the night. Ena's pale-blue sustenance shot through the branches, leaves, and forest floor, glowing brightly in the darkness. Nocturnal flowers and glowing fungi shone in all colours of the spectrum, as though they were trying to stand out against the unity of Ena's silver-blue hue. He paid no heed to the beauty around him, his mind set on a singular purpose. Using the memory of his dream and the inexplicable pull towards the edge of the forest, he knew exactly where he was headed. He was getting closer, somehow sensing the precise location of his destination. The urge was not just a memory, he realised. It was like a hook in his gut, tugging him along relentlessly, the sensation growing more urgent the closer he got.

It took a little longer than an hour at pace before he arrived. Keeping to the same level of forest, he clung to a branch. The edge of the trees spread out beside him in a uniform line of protection against the Abyss of the fields beyond. Like a sinister shadow in the bare light of the sliver of moon, the silhouette of the broken spire beyond was etched against the landscape.

He remembered learning about the Abyss for the first time as a boy, through the memories of the Hunters. Their teachings combined fear with a sense of vulnerability; no one travelled outside the shelter of the forests. Anyone wanting to visit Shadowspire far across these fields would, of course, take the long way around under cover of trees. No one dared to expose themselves outside the forest's protection. When Theren finally saw it with his own eyes, his fascination had outweighed his fear. Every time he'd visited thereafter, he had been alone or with Valyn. Where the others feared open space, he found himself strangely drawn to it. Not like the insistent tug he felt now, more a curiosity and wonder. Especially at night, the open fields were a beautiful mystery of muted colours, grass waving under the moonlight. For Valyn, they were the source of endless questions about the past that the Listeners guarded greedily.

Theren looked around, distracted as he tried to locate the source of the pull he felt. He ran the dream around his mind as his eyes searched the trees and branches, but he found no clues. The dream had been vague.

No. That was not true. In the dream, when he had stood at the edge of the forest, he had been on the ground. He leaped down from his branch and alighted on the forest floor. Somehow, he knew he stood exactly where he had in the dream.

There was nothing there, besides some crushed grass and a snapped twig on the ground. Of course there wasn't, he chastised himself. He'd had a strange dream and he was vastly overreacting. He crouched to examine the grass, running his hand through the dirt. There had been some sort of scuffle here; the ground was kicked up. He threw an orb of Light above him to better see, but the earth offered no answers.

Taking one last look around, he grabbed a low branch and swung himself back up into the trees. Higher he climbed until he found a comfortable position to look back out into the night. There was one more element of the dream he needed to check before he was satisfied.

He jumped across a few branches, searching for the symbol he'd seen in his mind. He found the sigil, just where it should be, carved into the trunk by ancestors even the Listeners seemed to have forgotten. It glowed with Ena's light, brightly as it ever did.

On his illicit trips to the edge of the forest, Theren had experimented with it, alternating between various ways of trying to take power from it or trying to siphon more of his power into it. The symbol had remained unchanged. Perhaps Valyn had a point, he thought. No one studied sigils in their own right. The Listeners were the only ones who recorded them, but that was simply an archive. Theren didn't even think anyone had invented a new sigil in years.

Out of a sense of duty, a connection he felt with his long-dead ancestors, Theren reached out and laid his hand against the ward again. He shifted Ena's light within him to touch the mark like he did as a boy. It flared briefly but did not change. Why would it? It had been an age since anyone remembered its purpose.

Though he had found no satisfaction and the tug in his stomach urged him to stay, he could not think of a reason. Theren turned and swung back into the forest. He was not eager to return to his bed, but he was less eager to call down the wrath of his elders for a prohibited trip out of the spire.

He sped back home, doing his best to remain undetected as he slunk through the city — mind quiet — keeping to roof, branch, or balcony rather than the main thoroughfares.

Back in his room, he undressed and sat by the warmheart in his nightgown and a robe. He leaned over the orb, holding his hands up to the glowing sphere. With a shift of power, he increased the warmth in an attempt to offset the shiver that ran down his spine. He repeated the dream over and over in his mind, unsatisfied that his journey had revealed nothing. He didn't know what he had been hoping to find, but something unsettled him.

The gnawing feeling in his stomach had not been alleviated.

It was nothing but a strange dream, he told himself. He was just over-tired and stressed about The Choosing and the Brotherwalk. It was nothing a good night's sleep couldn't fix.

He stood abruptly, waving a hand over the warmheart to dim the light before making his way to his bed. The Choosing was only a day away, and he wanted to be fresh.

Now was not the time for distraction; he had his future to face.

9

Dream Master Athas' disapproval was piercing as Theren hurried after his mother through the Dreamers' Tower door.

"He is too young," Athas protested. "It is not safe."

"You will do this," Ial replied, a thunderous force of will behind her words. Theren cringed, squeezing his eyes shut at her fury.

"I want to do it," Theren squeaked. Anything would be better than her rage. He peeked through one eye and saw Athas staring, stony-faced, at Ial. Surely no one would defy the order of the Speaker of Starspire?

"Very well," Athas said. Theren could feel nothing coming from him. "Theren will stay here tonight."

"Keep him for the day," Ial said, turning on her heel. "I want to be sure."

She left without looking back. Theren balled his hands into fists and tried not to show his trepidation on his face. He pushed it down deep, like he did all his other feelings.

Dream Master Athas' hand rested gently on his shoulder.

"You would be the youngest Dreamer to ever manifest," Athas said, sending out reassurance. "You've only just had your amulet taken off. I'm sure it is nothing." Theren tried not to think about how badly he didn't want to be a Dreamer. "Come." Athas pushed him gently through the foyer. "Tell me what you saw."

The day before The Choosing presented a conundrum; how would Theren spend his final day as a boy?

"You don't want to take Elsie, do you?" Ylia asked over breakfast while his niece was practising standing on her head in the middle of the room. Theren flicked his fingers and knocked her over with a gust of air, being sure to cushion her fall with his Light. Elska shrieked with delight while Ylia shook her head with a withering look.

I was thinking of spending today with friends, he answered the question with a thought that passed quicker than words could manage.

That would require you to have some.

Theren stuck his tongue out at her and proceeded to tidy up their meal. Perhaps a final day of being a reckless youth was what he needed. Last night's dream still simmered at the edge of his mind, and he needed a distraction. Perhaps he would see what his friends were doing, and maybe Valyn would like one final excursion up to the open air above the forest.

Yes, that would do. A rowdy day pretending to be a child, and then maybe he and Valyn could watch the sunset together.

Valyn, he reached out to her. She felt small, uncertain, and she pulled away from him. *What's wrong?* He sent his concern.

Nothing. Her lie was palpable. He could push, overtake her mind and find out for himself – and do it without her knowing — but that was something his mother would do. Theren dulled his thoughts and pulled himself inward instead. Just in case.

"Mother wants us to dine with her tonight," Ylia interrupted his train of thought. Theren thanked Ena for his foresight. He always suspected thinking about the Speaker somehow drew her attention.

"Why?" Theren replied, taking a toy from Elska as she brought it over to show him.

"It's the night before The Choosing," Ylia sent him a flicker of irritation, as though the reason was obvious. "She wants to celebrate."

Theren thought of a choice string of curse words but Ylia glared at him before he could voice them aloud.

Not in front of Elsie, you twit.

"Sorry," he replied. "But why? She never wants to see me unless it's to tell me off or judge me for something."

"She's not all bad," Ylia replied, emotionless.

Theren didn't argue. He didn't have to spend every day with their mother, shadowing her. Maybe there was a side to her he never saw.

He focused back on Valyn. Dinner with his mother and sister meant watching the sunset was no longer possible. *Want to watch the stars tonight?*

Fine, Valyn replied before shutting herself away.

Strange. Theren was tempted to push but decided against it. A person was entitled to their angst, and it was far from him to invade.

Besides, though he felt a little guilty, he was not overly eager for a day of Valyn's sour moods. This was his last day of childhood, and he intended to enjoy himself, especially if he had to see his mother that night.

His other friends delivered enjoyment in spades. A large group of them met in the lower levels of the city and spent the day getting up to mischief. They cleaned out a Grower's bakery, distracted the younger children in their lessons, and had vine fights at the top of the city — using their Light to control the plants as they attempted to knock each other off the branches. Every childish impulse they had ever acted on was relived; their joy enhanced for the knowledge it would be the last time they would ever be free to act as children. Their mirth and abandon intermingled, and Theren let himself be washed in their happiness.

None of them commented that Theren's emotions could not be felt, though he caught the edges of the occasional poorly guarded thought. *Selfish, to use the emotions of others without sharing your own,* one thought whispered. Theren made more of an effort to make his enjoyment known but he forgot to do it when he was deeply immersed in his fun.

Theren also held himself apart whenever the Brotherwalk was discussed. In just over a week, the men of every spire would leave, almost to the last of them, to journey to the other cities. Those left behind, the women, children, and the very elderly or infirm, would play host to men from all over Alvaren. It was a sacred, cultural rite, but the way it was discussed by his peers was with far more braggadocio than was proper. The boys boasted about their intended antics once they left Starspire, the girls making the appropriate interjections of disgust or teasing. Theren wished he could just become a Hunter and stay in the spire until he felt ready for the Brotherwalk. Such thoughts would mark him as more of a pariah than Valyn if anyone caught them, so he kept them locked away. He sent out fake mirth and laughter instead and hoped no one noticed how brittle it was.

At the end of the day, they all converged at Ena's spring, the girls and boys farewelling one another as they left to renew their Light in different pools.

When the light of the spire began to dim, he farewelled his friends and reached out to Valyn. Though he had a vague sense of her presence, he couldn't get a foothold in her mind. It was like she had suddenly learned to dull her thoughts entirely, shielding herself in a way she never had before.

He left her alone; he had to survive dinner with the Speaker. Best to clear all thoughts of Valyn before he had to face his mother. Her disapproval of their friendship was a fact of which he was oft reminded. Sometimes it seemed she disapproved of everything about him.

Fully restored with Light, he hurried back to his rooms and prepared himself. He neatly combed back the front lengths of his white hair and donned a fine, berry-red tunic, before he met Ylia in the foyer of her apartment.

"You might look like a man," Ylia teased, "but you'll always be my fool little brother." Theren grinned to prove her correct and she laughed. "Come," she said, wrapping her arm around his waist. "Let's see you out of childhood."

On his last night as a boy, he sat at the middle of a long, narrow glass table. His mother sat at one end, and Ylia at the other. He faced the open-air balcony, which spread out behind the gossamer drapes framing the doorway. The table was filled with the best delicacies of the Growers, including Theren's favourite sweet juice, all served with crystal platters and cutlery. The chandelier hovered low over the table, hundreds of small spheres each glowing with the light of the spire.

Ial held her narrow flute, the bubbles sending sparks above the glass. Light-imbued wine was a rare and special skill of the Growers, and Ial had a penchant for the tingle it caused on the tongue.

"A toast to our family's first and last Choosing." Ial smiled at Theren. How such a beautiful smile could seem so empty would remain a mystery, Theren decided behind masked thoughts.

He sent the appropriate sense of gratitude in her direction and adjusted his mind to feel for Ylia without looking at her. She was genuinely pleased for him, though she did not relate to his experience. As the Speaker's heir she had no need to sit through The Choosing when she had come of age five years prior.

"Thank you, Mother." Theren raised his own glass. Ylia did the same.

"I only hope your Profession is an honourable one," Ial added before taking a sip.

"The Hunters will offer him a place," Ylia insisted. The sharp sound of her cutlery sliding across her plate caused Theren to wince. Though they were rare, he hated these dinners, these farces of familial bonding. Surely Ial knew that, which was why she insisted on them.

"The Hunters would be a fine option for the son of the Speaker." Ial shared her approval as she dissected a plump red fruit with her knife and fork, the juices and seeds spilling out onto the plate. "The Builders want him, too, as do the Growers and the Listeners."

"You would be a good Listener, Theren." Ylia sent forth a flicker of encouragement with her words. Theren glanced at her, but she only had eyes for their mother.

"The Listeners are a fine Profession," Ial agreed with words, but the sense emanating from her was that their status was inadequate in her eyes. "But I think the Hunters will win their bid."

"All of the Professions are honourable." Theren bristled despite himself. "I am honoured to serve the spire in whichever way I am selected."

"Which you will do well, no doubt." The feeling from her as she spoke was more a threat than encouragement. His achievements and behaviour were a direct indictment on her, so she thought, even though she hardly had a thing to do with the man he had grown to be.

With a wave of her hand, Ial summoned the bottle of Light Wine from the centre of the table, fingers flicking as she tilted the bottle mid-air without ever touching it. She refilled her glass without spilling a drop, her ithlyn unchanged despite the effort.

Theren realised with shame that was something he would do, recalling Ylia's scolding at his bed-making the day before. Only someone with significant strength and control over their Light would use it in such a flippant manner. For most others, lifting an object without touching it and manoeuvring it in the void of space would require unreasonable Light expenditure and concentration. Theren could sense how much Light Ial called upon with the action, and it was negligible.

Theren inspected his mother's face as she sent the bottle back to the centre of the table. She was unreadable, but Theren knew she would never think about how her actions might be perceived. She was the Speaker; she could do what she liked.

Ial took a sip of her wine and set her gaze on Theren.

"Once you've embarked on your Brotherwalk you, too, can sample the delightful flavours of wine," she teased. Only adults were permitted certain pleasures of the spire.

"Not long now," Ylia said. "In just over a week we'll have the first Revel."

"How exciting," Ial sent forth her reserved enthusiasm. "Two grown children. You'll be able to get your own dwelling, my son. Surely you intend to take quarters within the Speaker's Tower?"

"I haven't-"

"No, of course you won't," Ial laughed. "Otherwise, it would be too hard to block me out. Like you did for most of today."

Her face was neutral but the feeling coming off her was nothing short of frightening.

Where were you? she spoke in his mind.

Despite himself, Theren glanced at Ylia for reassurance but was met with a furrowed brow and a sense of query.

Theren folded up his memories of the day; his raucous behaviour with his friends and, most importantly, his plans with Valyn after this dinner was done. He sent a placating reassurance in both directions of the table.

"I was with my friends."

Why was his mother so controlling? He couldn't have a day to himself without her taking advantage of her ability to invade his mind? His supressed the surge of frustration in his gut.

"No one knew where you were until I suddenly felt you at Ena's spring with the others." Ylia spoke this time.

"Why were you looking for me?"

Ial sipped from her glass as Ylia answered. "I wasn't, particularly, I just began to notice your absence after a while."

"Were you with Valyn today?" Ial asked, her tone measured.

"No." Though it was true, he sounded guilty.

"I heard Valyn was with you down by the pools a few days ago when you renewed yourself after the Hunt," Ial accused.

"Theren." Ylia's sigh was intermingled with her exasperation. Theren shot back irritation. Ylia of all people knew what Valyn meant to him.

"She was just welcoming me home." He looked to his mother.

Ial set down her cutlery.

"Theren, many young men feel they cannot wait until the Brotherwalk to fulfil certain desires-" Theren's squirming embarrassment was so instant, he didn't manage to hide it "-but you know it is inappropriate to choose a lover from your own spire —"

"That is *not* —"

"-and of all the girls you could choose, Valyn should not even warrant a place on your list."

Ial settled her unnervingly emotionless gaze on him.

Strangely, he felt the need to defend Valyn's value as a romantic partner, even if he did not feel that type of interest in her.

"Anyone would be lucky to have Valyn as their partner, Mother. You just have a narrow idea of what constitutes value."

"Well, in a few months' time you'll be gone and another will take your place, if that aberrant girl can keep her obstinate mouth shut for long enough."

Ial returned to her meal and Ylia's flash of warning in Theren's mind was almost blinding.

Let it go.

She was right. It would be foolish to do anything to raise his mother's ire further. He buried his impotent rage so deep it filled his stomach and he lost his appetite.

They continued eating in silence, Theren waiting on edge for the next thing Ial would bring up. There was always something more. Perhaps she'd sensed his weapons practise with Valyn, or his trepidation each time someone mentioned the acts required on the Brotherwalk.

He cut himself off from all feeling entirely when the memory of that strange dream floated behind his eyes. Please, *please* don't let her have noticed that, he begged Ena.

Ena appeared to answer his plea, for the meal continued in relative calm; Ial content to ask minimally antagonistic questions and seemingly only mildly dissatisfied that she never got a rise from him. How desperately Theren wanted to get out of the Speaker's Tower, out of the spire altogether, and into the freedom of the open sky.

Once dinner was over and he was in his room, he locked away the residual black anger and reached out to Valyn. He could scarcely feel her, but the parts of her he could were filled with trepidation and fear.

Oh Valyn, he murmured in her mind. *Whatever happens tomorrow at The Choosing will be fine. It is up to Ena.* She didn't respond. *It doesn't matter to me whether you have a Profession,* he placated. She was non-responsive, the sense of her emotion gone too.

He supposed he would be watching the stars alone tonight. His eyes fell on his bed in the dim light of his room, the temptation of a soft mattress and warm covers calling to him.

And yet, another call was louder; the pull towards the edge of the forest that he had managed to ignore all day. The image of the sigil floated behind his eyes as he again recalled the dream, as clear now as it had been the night before.

His comfortable bed could wait. He was eager to watch the stars.

Theren left his room like a silent ghost, not even bothering to change into his armour. The forest knew him, and he it, and he was unafraid of what lived within. He flew through the trees until he emerged at the edge of the forest where he had found himself the other night.

The open plain stretched before him, the starry sky above.

And a strange gnawing in his stomach, which was surely just nerves for tomorrow.

10

Theren stood in the hall of the Speaker's Tower beside the Dream Master, keeping stone-still despite the dread in his stomach. Ial barely looked at him, in contrast to the passers-by, who had stopped on the stairs to gawk.

"He is not a Dreamer, Speaker," Dream Master Athas reassured his leader. "The dream he had seems nothing more than a boyish nightmare."

Relief flooded him and he glanced at his mother. She remained cold.

"Good. That will be all then." Without looking at him, she directed Theren to his room with a thought. He skittered away like a deer. The Dream Master told him he'd just had a nightmare and there was nothing to worry about. He'd never been more relieved of anything in his life. He didn't want to be a Dreamer;

they were strange. Everyone knew the stories of their failure all those centuries ago; the Mad Dreamer's fate was known in every spire in Alvaren. Yet, though the Dream Master had reassured him that his dream was normal, he couldn't shake the ominous feeling that something was amiss.

He shook his head as he hurried home. It was nothing.

Yet, he still hoped his mother didn't go on the Speakerswalk that year.

Most parents would walk their children to The Choosing but Theren walked through the spire alone. Ial would be leading the proceedings, and Ylia, as her apprentice, would be by her side. Roshin would be taking Valyn, and though part of him had hoped the two of them would summon him to join them, their minds had been silent that morning. He told himself he wasn't hurt by it.

The Choosing was held at one of the several gathering places in the city, an amphitheatre in the shape of a broad crystal bowl that appeared to hover between Ena's trunk and the pillars of the spire's towers. It was held aloft by the sigils of the builders and linked to the spire itself by narrow bridges, like strings of spider's silk. A soft glow emanated from within the glass, as it did across the spire, and the layers of canopy above twinkled like stars.

The boys and girls sat among the first rows, separated by the centre aisle, a semi-circular arc of hopes, and dreams, and fears. By this age, everyone was practised at quietening their minds, but the sense of anticipation practically blurred the air between them as they awaited the Masters to call on them.

In the rows above, the parents, relatives, and onlookers from across the spire had come to see what the future held for their people; who among the newest generation of adults would join the ranks of the Professions, and who would be relegated to the insignificance of the common folk. Not every job was a Profession, such as Roshin's labour in serving the Speaker, and while these jobs were valued, they were certainly not held with the same prestige. Only the most powerful and skilled with their Light were Profession material.

Theren sat in the thick of nervous jokes and over-stuffed laughter, only a few places away from the centre aisle. Directly on the other side of the aisle sat Valyn, the girl beside her leaving a noticeable gap between them. Dressed in a dark green gown, her short, pale hair pinned back with a decorative clip of glowing green gemstones, Valyn looked almost as normal as everyone else. No doubt Roshin had bullied her into wearing a dress. Unlike everyone else, who was whispering and gossiping with excitement, Valyn sat with a drawn expression, staring forward like she was lost in thought.

Beside her, the girls talked, appearing unbothered by the currents of fate flowing around them. Despite their outward appearance, Theren could feel the anxiety hidden by such carefree conversation. He watched Valyn, who sat in stony-faced silence, and felt a twist of worry in his stomach on her behalf. It was unlikely she would be Chosen today, despite her aptitude in a range of subjects. She would have made a fine Grower, what with Roshin's talents, but she would have thrived among the Listeners most of all.

Alas, few Professions were eager for a troublemaker who just didn't quite fit in. She was not the kind of person the people of Starspire wished for a leader, even though he rather thought she was the kind of person they needed. As far as the Listeners recalled, Alvar culture had remained unchanged since the Void were defeated a millennia ago. Theren sometimes wondered whether society would grow stagnant without something to alter their ways. The leaders of Starspire, his mother included, seemed content to keep things as they had always been.

Those very same leaders filed down the aisle to stand in front of the crowd in an orderly line, the six heads of the Professions who served the Speaker on her council. Theren watched them all, his eyes lingering on Hunt Master Feldan. His own place among them was all but guaranteed.

His gaze fell on Dream Master Athas next. There was one Profession to which he knew he was not called, and the thought brought him no small measure of relief. Athas was there only in a ceremonial capacity. The Dreamers had already selected their ilk over the years, or more correctly, Ena had selected them and the Dreamers unearthed them. The curse of Dreaming came unpredictably and required immediate admission to the Dreamers' Tower so the chosen child could learn to control their skill.

Theren smiled inwardly as he remembered the day after Valyn's own testing; she had arrived at lessons with unbrushed hair and an expression of bleary-eyed anger on her face. The Dreamers took children seemingly at random for testing, according to their secretive, mysterious rules. Ial hated that they were unpredictable in this regard. It was a process over which she had no control.

Theren's thoughts were interrupted by a powerful presence in his mind.

People of Starspire, came the Speaker's voice, accompanied by a sense of control that could not be ignored. It silenced the crowd in a moment; alluring, authoritative, absolute.

He looked up to see his mother descending from a bridge opposite the seating. Ylia followed at a respectful five paces behind.

The Speaker's council, the men and women standing patiently in front of the crowd, turned and formed two orderly lines for the Speaker to walk between. Theren blended his mind with the crowd around him and saw through their eyes for a moment. The Speaker, her wisdom unquestionable and her power unmatched, made her way with a measured stride. She was a vision of Alvar perfection and Ena's Light all in one — tall, slender, hair as pale as her white-blue eyes. Her ithlyn shone brightly against her fair skin, her lips a red stain in her unmarked face. Her expression was perfectly neutral.

Theren shut himself away again, the awe and admiration in his chest fading fast. In this, he did not share his people's views. He glanced at Valyn who, he knew, was the only other aware of the truth. It was not only *her* memories they had shared as little ones with hands wrapped over amulets.

Today is a momentous day, Ial spoke in their minds. *Today we welcome a new generation into adulthood. Today the spire is strengthened with the talents of our young ones.*

An impression of Starspire formed in Theren's mind, moving as though time had sped up. In the moment it took to blink, he watched as Starspire changed and glowed brighter, the forest lighting up in pride. Ena's love for them was all-consuming.

Theren shook his head slightly as the image cleared. It was not the forest, or Ena, they were feeling. Ial was controlling their emotions. She was so powerful that none in the crowd — not even Theren — could inhibit the visions and feelings she created for them during her speech. As one, they lived the first moments of a mother as she looked upon her newborn child, the next they watched with hearts in their throats as their children first learned to climb among the boughs of the forest. They weathered tantrums, relived bedtime stories, and witnessed first days of school.

Theren hated that there were tears welling in his eyes at the swell of indescribable emotion in his chest; a love so deep it hurt. These could not be Ial's memories; surely, she had stolen them from the countless mothers in the spire. Perhaps that was what Roshin had felt when she had held Valyn.

"And now our children stop being our children and become our peers instead," Ial concluded aloud, letting her grip on their minds fade. Theren blinked away his tears and glanced around. The girls on the other side of the aisle were openly crying, and the boys were all wiping their cheeks. Sniffles could be heard throughout the audience.

Theren pulled his mind in on itself and tried to quell the hot surge that ran through him. It wasn't right that one person could control the thoughts of so many people. He glanced at Valyn again but she was looking at the ground. A strong trepidation lay behind the maternal sadness Ial had implanted in her.

Valyn was right to be angry at the way things were. Those with power simply had to be trusted; there was no way of checking their control over others.

"It is time." Ial spoke aloud now. "Head Builder Imbryl." She introduced the leader of the Builders and the man stepped forward. Theren tensed as the thrum of energy shifted with anticipation. Anxiety vibrated around him. The Professions would have already discussed their selections, deciding collectively who would be best placed in which Profession. According to Ylia, the top students were bargained for; if you let us have Talis, the Growers might say to the Weavers, you can have both Rys and Ithala.

Head Builder Imbryl sent forth a small flicker of calm and stated his first selection aloud. Only the Speaker had the power to speak in the minds of the whole spire without raising a sweat.

"Carana, daughter of Roselyn."

Theren looked to the girls' side of the aisle where Cara stood with a flow of pride. Her friends trilled with congratulations as Cara stepped onto the stage and bowed to Head Builder Imbryl. The audience sent forth the wave of congratulations, and Theren sent his too.

Head Builder Imbryl stated several more names, and the Chosen joined him on the stage one by one. Though the outward response from the crowd was silence, in the minds of those present there was a cacophony of warmth and celebration. Imbryl finished his list of names. Neither Theren nor Valyn was among them. Theren was relieved. He hoped Hunt Master Feldan had won whatever debate was needed to take him.

The leader of the Listeners stepped up next and began her list. Theren allowed himself a moment of hope for Valyn. The Listeners were objective recorders of history, but truly no-one could be objective. Valyn had protested as such when they were first learning their arts as children. Since true objectivity could not be managed, Valyn had argued, surely all different types of people should be Listeners?

Despite Theren's belief in her, none of the names that echoed around the amphitheatre were Valyn's. None were Theren's either, but that wasn't surprising. It would be Feldan who called his name that day.

He glanced over to Valyn, where she had put her head in her hands.

I'm sorry, Val, he sent out to her. He knew she had been holding out for the Listeners. If she heard him, she did not show it. She simply remained silent, her mind closed off and her face hidden.

The Growers were next, then the Weavers. Neither Theren's nor Valyn's names were called, but plenty of his friends departed. Theren sent out his congratulations each time with a carefully controlled face.

Finally, and last of all, Hunt Master Feldan stepped forward and began his list of names. Theren sat up straight, heart thrumming with anticipation.

"Theren, son of Ial."

A chorus of pride and joy rang through the minds of the crowd, Theren feeling it all. He stood to receive the adulation. Everything he'd ever wanted and worked so hard for had led to this moment. It almost felt like a dream. Not like the dream the other night, which still niggled at him with an uncanny clarity. This felt hazy, dizzying, and he stumbled down to the stage to receive Feldan's Choosing, doing everything he could to stop himself from grinning.

He stood beside the Hunt Master as several other names were called, all boys, of course. Theren couldn't help but glance at Valyn. She never even had a chance to stand beside him, even though she would have been a good Hunter. She was fearless, and brave, and near as good with her knives as he was. He tried to hide his guilt and simply enjoy the moment. It wasn't his fault the world was unfair.

Feldan finished calling his names and Theren took in the faces of his newest brethren, the group of them sending a warm approval among themselves before retaking their seats. It was done. The Choosing was over.

Time to focus on the Brotherwalk and his months-long journey out of the spire. Theren sighed and rested his elbow on his knee. The Revel would be in a week's time and...

His thoughts trailed off as Dream Master Athas stepped forward.

"I have one Choosing to make," he stated matter-of-factly. Consternation rippled through the crowd. An icy hand grabbed Theren's heart and he looked frantically at Valyn. She lifted her head and looked at him. She had been crying.

Dread coursed through him.

"Valyn, daughter of Roshin," Athas declared in his stony voice.

This time, the murmur from the crowd was audible. Valyn stood and made her way to the stage with her head hanging.

11

Valyn looked like an angry siryl whose nest of seeds had been disturbed when she appeared at school late that morning.

What's wrong? Theren asked in her mind as she sat down, knowing Teacher Leana would not overhear. She never seemed to notice when he spoke to his classmates.

Valyn didn't answer, either aloud or in his mind, but she didn't need to. Her exhaustion and frustration thrummed through her classmates, overlaid with flashes of the Dreamers' Tower.

She must have been tested last night.

Theren recalled his own night in the Dreamers' Tower, fear turning his stomach. Everyone who'd sat through it looked exhausted afterwards. Those who were still to be tested spoke of it with dread. All must face the Dreamers' examination in case the skill — or curse — was manifesting. It was the only Profession that took apprentices before they came of age.

Dreams didn't follow the rules.

Theren tried to get to Valyn after The Choosing but he was mobbed by the crowd congratulating him on his newfound Hunter status.

Hunter Theren, they called him. The title he'd coveted since he was a boy. The title Valyn had yearned for but could never be hers. Would never be hers now, even if she managed to change the rules of the spire. She was a Dreamer, doomed to life in the Dreamers' Tower. How could this happen? Valyn had been tested as a child and showed no manifestation of Dreaming. It wasn't right.

By the time Theren finally extricated himself from the crowd, Valyn was gone, and Theren's frustration threatened to boil over.

Where are you? he called to her. She was cloudy, her physical whereabouts hard to locate. There was only one place she could be. Theren set his jaw and set off for the Dreamers' Tower, fear and fury burning in his gut.

Don't, came Roshin's warning in his mind. *Just leave her be. She is with Athas.*

Leave her? Theren sent his outrage.

A vision of a familiar kitchen swam behind his eyes, an urn of steaming tisane on the table. Theren sighed and changed course for Roshin's.

She waited for him at the door of her little vine-covered home, just like she had when he was a boy returning home after lessons. A pang hit him, a nostalgia so melancholy he felt his throat tighten. Roshin pulled him into an embrace.

"How has this happened?" he murmured into her hair, his chin atop her head.

"Come inside, love." Though Roshin's lip quivered, she kept her face impassive. Theren was not a child anymore, after all, and physical expressions were no longer appropriate. Theren longed to see her smile.

"I hate this," he said as he slumped into the chair. Roshin poured him a steaming cup of redfruit and he wrapped his fingers around it, seeking its warm comfort. "This isn't right. How?"

Roshin sighed as she eased herself into her seat. "I don't know. Athas came yesterday and told us he'd caught Valyn Dreaming the night before. He took her to the Tower right away."

"How does he know?"

Roshin shared her own confusion. "The Dreamers' secrets are not for us to understand."

For the first time, Theren understood his mother's controlling ways. When it came to his friend, he would do almost anything to know what was going on.

"Is she alright?" Theren asked, already knowing the answer. Of course, she wasn't. She already thought herself a pariah. This would only confirm it. She had been strange her whole life, only to end up as a Dreamer on the day of The Choosing. Plucked from the crowd in front of everyone.

"She will be alright," Roshin reassured him. "The Dreamers are as important as any other job in the spire. We all serve Ena."

Theren felt her conviction, though he did not agree. Whatever value the Dreamers had in making predictions about the future was rarely shared with common citizens. Likewise, their visions of the past were only shared if the Listeners and the Speaker's Council saw fit. But, unlike everyone else who quietly dismissed the Dreamers whilst paying lip service to their value, Roshin believed what she was saying.

"Dreamer Athas was a friend of your mother's when we were children," Roshin continued. "He was beloved. Handsome, powerful, popular; I even wonder sometimes if your mother didn't wish he lived in another spire so she could..."

Theren sent her a sharp reminder of his presence. Roshin must have forgot herself, for she smiled over her cup.

"Sorry. Anyway, we all thought he'd grow up to be a Hunter. But then one day he never turned up for lessons. We didn't see him for weeks."

This was common. Most times, when a Dreamer was uncovered, they remained in the Dreamers' Tower for several weeks, sometimes months, before they were seen in the spire again. Only the Dreamers knew why.

"The rest is history, as the Listeners would say," Roshin sipped her tisane. Theren waited, sensing her story was not yet done. "When Athas emerged, everyone treated him differently. But why? He was the same boy, just with a new purpose. I never understood why we shun them so."

Theren knew why. The warnings about Dreaming were told regularly around the glow of warmhearts amidst the other Listener stories.

Undiscovered, unchecked, a Dreamer could go mad. And, as Valyn herself had once joked, all the Dreamers did was 'expert sleeping,' as far as she was concerned.

"I'm sad for Valyn," Roshin concluded. "But only because she is sad. This is just Ena's will."

Ena's will. As was everything, he supposed. It was Ena's will that some were cursed with Dreaming, that his mother was a tyrant, that he would be separated from his dearest friend when he left on his Brotherwalk, not even able to spend his final week in the spire with her.

"Roshin," Theren blurted. "I don't want to go on the Brotherwalk." He didn't know why he told her, but this day was all wrong. It seemed as good a time as any to defy expectation. He sent her his shame, and her face broke from impassivity to pity.

"Oh, Theren. You are brave and skilled." She took his hand as she searched his face. "But...you're not afraid of the journey..."

Though Theren's instinct was to withdraw into himself, he relaxed his mind. He wanted someone to understand. He wished he'd told Valyn. It was so lonely, keeping your thoughts to yourself all the time.

"You're afraid of the destination," Roshin breathed. He felt the fleeting edge of memories with a heart-fluttering thrill before Roshin veiled her mind again, no doubt locking away experiences unsuitable for sharing with the young man she thought of as her son.

"How are we supposed to do it all?" he continued. "Find someone we like, who likes us, too, and then trust them enough to...to...reveal ourselves...?" Theren trailed off, his cheeks burning. Hunter Theren, they might call him now, but he was just a coward.

"You're not a coward," Roshin scolded, though amusement tinged her words. Theren glared at her.

"It's not funny!"

Roshin leaned back and took a sip of her tisane. "It's a little bit funny. You're utterly fearless when you're staring down an ogyr and traversing the forests for weeks, yet the thought of speaking to a strange woman..." She trailed off, and he felt her mind wander.

"I don't want to leave Valyn now," Theren changed the subject, folding his thoughts back into themselves. He thought Roshin of all people would've understood. "She needs me."

Roshin placed her cup down with a sharp 'clink' on the crystal table and fixed him a serious expression. Her amusement had evaporated, replaced with concern.

"Do you fear the Brotherwalk because you want to be with a man instead?"

"What?" Theren's shock leaked past his mental barrier. "No! Is that even allowed?"

"No, but that doesn't mean it doesn't happen," Roshin replied matter-of-factly. "Second question. Do you want to be with Valyn like the women on the Brotherwalk?"

"No!" Theren recoiled in horror. "I love her, truly, but not like that." He released his mind, sending Roshin a litany of memories to prove his honesty; the moments playing with Valyn on the floor of her room, getting her out of trouble, standing up for her when their classmates taunted her temper — moment on moment of fierce loyalty and inseparable familiarity. Familiarity like sharing Valyn's bed with their hands over each other's amulets when they were small and, when they were older, falling asleep with their minds open to one another, intertwined. Just like they had the other night.

"What?" Roshin stood up so fast her chair moved back with a screech on the glass floor. "What happened the other night?"

Theren looked up at her and blinked. "What do you mean?"

"You fell asleep with your minds interlinked?"

"Valyn had a bad day...I was-"

Roshin leaned close to him. "What night?"

With his stomach turning cold for the second time that day, Theren remembered the dream. The tug in his gut swelled, calling him to the edge of the forest with the recollection of the memory. The sigil flared and burned in his mind's eye.

"The night Valyn had the dream."

They stared at each other, the only sound the gentle tapping of the vines on the kitchen window.

12

It was happening again.

Theren blinked and suddenly he was standing in his room. Where had he come from? Fear sparked through him, and he ran to his bed and pulled the covers around him as he tried to orient himself. He closed his eyes and used his Light to form a bubble around him. What had he been doing? Where had he been?

Why did he forget things all the time?

An echo of anger returned to him; his? Yes, he realised, he was angry. He had been angry. But then the anger morphed and warped into someone else's. Mother's. And it was not just anger, no, it was a fury unmatched; a force of nature. He wondered who the true Entity in Starspire was — Ena or his mother.

He did not recall why he had been angry or what had transpired between the two of them. This was not the first time such a thing had happened, and he had come to learn that it was futile trying to recall it. Knowing now he was not in danger, he pulled his Light back into himself and let the covers drop. He opened his eyes and looked around his room. The shock and anger subsided, making way for a new fear. A colder, slower anxiety that curled around his heart.

Why did he forget things all the time? Was there something wrong with his mind?

The Dreamers' Tower was a singular, narrow spear of crystal that jutted up beside a colossal tree. It was entirely windowless except for the highest level, where delicate arches ringed the upper floor. The impenetrable visage of the opaque monolith reminded Theren of the rarely used prison hidden beneath the city, though that was more dirt and tree roots than glass. Two large doors of dark crystal, engraved with pale blue sigils, loomed in front Theren and Roshin as they stood outside. Roshin held Theren's hand, sending him a constant trickle of reassurance. Theren chose to ignore the worry she was trying to hide from him. He had enough of his own.

Roshin rested her hand on the doors, and Theren felt a flash of Light pass between her and the sigils. She stepped back and waited.

"What are we doing?" Theren asked, sending out his impatience. Why hadn't Roshin reached out to Athas on their way?

"They can't hear us in there," she explained. "And we can't hear them."

She pointed to the sigils. Theren recognised some of them as those that controlled the forces of movement, but there were several other foreign ones too.

"That's why I couldn't sense Val properly," Theren murmured to himself.

Imagine how I feel, Roshin replied with a twinge of anxiety.

The doors opened to reveal Dream Master Athas standing on the other side. Theren considered Roshin's words about the man in his youth; he had, himself, often thought that the Dream Master looked like the farthest thing from a Dreamer. He was broad and muscular, and he held himself with a sure-footed grace that would have better suited the armour of the Hunters than the dark, flowing robes he wore now. His pale blue eyes fell on

Theren, his thick white braids arranged on his shoulders.

"Roshin," he said in a deep timbre. He looked at Theren. "And Speakerson." Roshin and Theren both offered the Alvar bow, which Athas returned. "Something is wrong?" Athas asked Roshin.

"Valyn may not be your Dreamer," Roshin replied, getting straight to the point.

Theren tried not to hope that she was, tried not to think that Valyn was better suited for the role. She was already an outcast, and her mother loved her either way. But his hope remained, despite the shame he felt. He hung his head and sent forth a hint of unease.

"We are not measured by our first thoughts," Dreamer Athas spoke, as though he'd heard Theren's inner turmoil. He rested his hand on Theren's shoulder. "But by what we do in spite of them."

Theren looked up into Athas' kind face, a calm strength emanating from the man. Something in Theren's stomach grew; a pull towards the edge of the forest, a flash of a sigil behind his eyes.

"Roshin, I think you might be right," Athas said, confused concern palpable behind his words. "Things have not proceeded here as they should since Valyn joined us. I think we need to talk." Athas turned away as Roshin stepped after him. "Come, Theren," Athas encouraged when he did not move. Theren followed at a trudge, wincing as the doors closed behind him.

Valyn sat on the edge of a bed in a small, windowless room, another empty bed beside her. The glow of Ena's Light emanated from the opaque glass walls, and the smooth floor was covered in a simple, woven rug of midnight blue. Theren remembered being in a similar room when he'd been tested as a boy. Her eyes were red as she looked up; shock registering across her face for a moment when she laid eyes on him.

"Theren!"

Theren hurried to her side and pulled her into an embrace. Roshin followed close behind, wrapping her arms around them both.

"I'm so sorry," Theren murmured.

Valyn pulled away from him and looked at Athas as she squeezed her mother's hand. "What's going on? What is Theren doing here?"

Athas folded his hands together and remained inexpressive. "Theren? Perhaps you wish to explain. I, too, would like to understand what has happened."

Theren glanced at Valyn and folded his hands nervously, tracing over his ithlyn with his fingertips. She narrowed her eyes, still as expressive as a child despite the fact that they now both held titles and the Dream Master himself was standing before them.

"The other night, Valyn and I fell asleep with our minds together. I think we had the same dream."

Theren explained that night to Athas; from the moment he reached out to Valyn, to his false awakening, to the dream itself. He omitted his illicit venture out of the spire and that the feeling still pushed at him, urging him back to the edge of the forest.

Athas' consternation was palpable while Valyn just stared at him, her eyes and thoughts conveying fear and confusion in equal measure.

"I...I could barely remember the dream," she stammered. She looked at Athas. "See? I wasn't lying."

"I knew you weren't lying," Athas replied, which was no doubt true. She was less skilled at hiding her feelings than Theren. "I was as confused as you."

Valyn clutched her hand to her chest. "It wasn't really my dream."

Her relief leaked through even as Theren's trepidation grew.

"No," Athas agreed. "Perhaps it wasn't." He turned to Theren. "But we must be sure. Theren, please show me the dream."

Theren rested his hands on his knees and conjured his memory of the dream, sending it to Athas. He tried to run through it as orderly as possible, starting at the beginning and slowing it down, hiding his emotional reactions to the dream as it unfolded. Throughout, the pull towards the edge of the forest grew, urging him to leave and run, run to the Abyss again. He needed to be there. Just like he had been on the night of the Dream.

Fearing Athas would notice the feeling, he closed his mind away; buried deep until his head was empty and he felt nothing. He did not want to reveal he had ventured into the forest that night.

Theren? Athas' voice seemed to echo in his mind.

Yes?

Where...where are your memories? Where is the dream?

Theren held Athas' gaze, ignoring Valyn shifting beside him.

What do you mean?

ATHAS! A third, familiar voice joined them through Athas' mind; not intended for Theren but sent with such force he heard it anyway. His mind buried itself deeper.

"We're about to have company." Athas looked to Valyn. "But you, Valyn, are not a Dreamer. I am sorry for hastily bringing you here. I was worried that a showing this late would mean your risk of Dreamers madness was greater."

"Madness?" Theren interjected, but Athas didn't respond.

Valyn leapt to her feet and hurried to her mother's side. Roshin put her arm around her. "What should I tell people?" Valyn asked.

"Nothing, yet. Now, go. I suspect you'd prefer to be far away when the Speaker joins us."

Valyn and Roshin each gave Theren a long look before they left the room.

"Your mother is requesting we join her in the Speaker's Tower," Athas explained, his tone perfectly neutral. No doubt Ial was deafening the Dream Master with her demands. "But I think it would be best if she came here." His frustration flared. "There is a lot to explain, and we don't have time."

"We should do what she says," Theren replied. "It's worse when you refuse."

"Perhaps," Athas replied. "But her power is limited in the Tower. For example, you've not heard her calling to you at all, have you?"

"No, but that's not unusual. She regularly complains that she can't find me, and then sends Ylia out to interrogate my friends."

Athas sent him a shimmer of understanding. "Ah, I think that explains some things. Still, I will insist that she joins us here. She might be the Speaker, but we are the ones who truly know Ena."

"What?" Theren asked. The Speaker, as the name suggested, was the spire's conduit with their Entity.

Athas swept from the room without addressing the statement, indicating Theren should follow. Theren hurried after him.

It was not Ial's presence that Theren first felt as he waited in the Dreamers' foyer, but his sister's. He reached out to her, flaring his Light slightly to push through the sigils that prevented communication outside of the Tower. He felt her cling to him.

Ren, Ylia's voice spoke in his mind, though their connection was difficult to hold. He got the sense she was hurrying through the spire after their mother. *What's going on? I can barely feel you.*

Judging words to be inadequate, Theren simply conjured up the memory of the night of the dream and fragments of the recent conversation between he, Athas, and Valyn. He held it in his mind for only a moment, letting it slide away before anyone could overhear. Ylia did not reply with words, but he felt her trepidation and confusion. They let each other go.

The foyer was beautiful, with a seemingly infinite ceiling and a crystal staircase that spiralled up to landings leading to the rest of the tower's rooms. Shining spheres of pale blue floated in the void above, enhancing the light cast by the glow of the walls. Theren would have admired the work of the Builders were he not fighting the knot in his stomach. He shivered, suddenly cold.

Ial burst through the front door a moment later, her lips drawn and her fury akin to a rioting mob.

Have courage, Ren, Ylia whispered. Theren hardly heard her.

Ial slammed the doors closed behind her with a wave of her hand, not bothering to use the sigils. Ylia waited in the alcove of the entrance, seemingly fearful to come closer. Ial glared at Athas, who held her gaze, and Theren could sense their silent but furious frenzy of communication. Long moments passed without a word spoken aloud, and Theren realised they were conversing about him. A surge of anger rose in his throat. Were they really discussing this without him? The person this ultimately affected most? He shot his irritation toward the two of them. Ial rounded on him, and he instantly regretted his temper.

"Leave here, Theren, and wait for me in my room." Her anger burned through him.

"I don't think I can." Theren looked at Athas.

"Your son is a Dreamer," Athas said calmly. The words didn't quite sound real.

"He is not." Ial's voice was icy.

"I had a strange dream the other night," Theren said.

"He is *not* to be a Dreamer, Athas," Ial commanded, ignoring her son.

"Neither you nor I decide that, Speaker. Ena decides," Athas replied, his energy calm even in the face of the Speaker's rage, rage that suddenly flared like the light from a warmheart.

"You think to dictate Ena's will to me?"

"I don't dictate anything. I'm simply saying what you already know to be true."

Theren eyed Dreamer Athas and decided that if he could have even half of the man's self-possession then maybe he would be content to be a Dreamer. He tried to emulate the feeling within himself.

"The Revel is in a week," Ial said. "Then the Brotherwalk."

"Why does that matter?" Theren interjected. Athas sent him an apologetic twinge that explained everything; Theren would not be leaving for the Brotherwalk. "But why not?" Theren asked, amplifying his disappointment. He might have dreaded some elements of the Brotherwalk but it would be worse to be stuck in this in-between stage of half man, half boy, in a Profession he didn't want.

"We cannot allow you to leave on the Brotherwalk until we are certain you can manage your Dreams," Athas explained.

"Normally, we would have trained you by now, but circumstances being what they are..." Athas returned his gaze to Ial "Perhaps if you had not brought him to me so young-"

Ial took a step forward, her ithlyn flashing as she called a hot wind up behind her, her fury taking physical form.

"You dare blame me?"

Athas, his robe rippling in the breeze, his white braids blasted from his shoulders, simply folded his hands behind his back.

"I am hypothesising."

As suddenly as it blew through, the wind stopped.

"The other spires know the Speaker's Son of Starspire is due his Brotherwalk this year," Ial hissed. "Everyone, in every spire, will be looking for Theren, son of Ial. I will not have people speak of a half-man *Dreamer*" — she nearly spat the word — "in relation to me."

"I am telling you what needs to be done," Athas replied. "The risk of Dreamers madness is ever-present. You know this, Speaker. Dreams warp reality. They erode our ability to tell memory and premonition from present experience. Without the proper training, he will be unable to tell what is Dream and what is real. He will go mad. Is that what you want people to say about the son of the Speaker of Starspire?"

"Is that true?" Theren tried to interject, but Ial spoke over the top of him.

"You can teach him to control it, and he can continue to another Profession after," she stated, as though she dictated all the rules of the spire. She might be the law but she did not control the natural forces of the world, try as she might.

"That is not possible," Athas replied with a sense of impatience. Ial returned the emotion with a wave of hostility. "Speaker." Athas levelled a wave of deep concern at them both. "If you prevent Theren from joining us, he may die."

Theren stomach iced over. Die?

Why? he asked Athas directly.

There are few good conclusions to the madness of an uncontrolled Dreamer, Theren.

Theren's heart raced, his breathing fast, and his eyes examined the crystal floor. He had hastened here to clear Valyn's name, but had never thought so far ahead to predict he would be standing here, his Dreamer status all but concluded, learning of his death if he were to deny it. There was no time to make sense of it. He truly had no choice. This was his future. He wouldn't have to worry about finding a lover while on his Brotherwalk now, he thought wryly; everyone would surely avoid him once he revealed his Profession.

He looked up at his mother, her cold gaze upon him. He pushed against her mind and realised she was considering his death as the better option. Better the condolences to a grieving mother than the whispers about a Dreaming half-man of a son.

A helpless rage swept through him.

With as much force as he could muster, he rushed forth a wave of anger, betrayal, and hurt at his mother as loudly as he could. She took a step backwards, shock briefly flickering across her stern face.

"I will stay here, Dreamer Athas." Theren straightened his back. "I will become a Dreamer. I will move into the tower tonight."

"No." Ial glared at him.

"Yes. It's my choice. I'm no longer a boy, and you do not control me."

Ial held his gaze and an intense pressure built in his head. Her presence pushed against his mind. His ithlyn flared as he resisted her, but he was no match. She leaked through, a force swarming, altering. His conviction faltered. Perhaps she was right? He didn't want to be a Dreamer; he'd never wanted it. Who would? He was a Hunter, declared just today at The Choosing. He was so proud; the thing he'd wanted all his life now in the palm of his hand. Perhaps he would even be Hunt Master one day. And surely, all the women of every spire would want him; the Brotherwalk would be a journey of thrill in every way; surviving the forest and resting in the arms of...

A small hint of terror, the emotion truly his own, screamed in the back of his mind. Surely Ial was not doing this...this forbidden thing...in the presence of others?

Then, with a sudden emptiness, she was gone. His own emotion rushed back into him; fear, shame, rage — all with such force his hands trembled. He blinked, staring at his mother, whose silent shock was a stark contrast to her loud fury of moments ago. Theren looked to Athas, who seemed none the wiser. Theren tried to block his mind, tried to suppress the fear, but for once, he felt laid bare. Raw.

Body shaking, Theren looked to Ylia, who stood by the door with her hands clenched in fists, breathing heavily. The delicate lines of her ithlyn were dim.

"Speaker. Mother," she said, eyes on Ial. "If Theren is a Dreamer, and accepts this fate, we must bend to the will of Ena."

Ial's ithlyn glowed a little less brightly, and there was a void where her presence had been only a moment ago.

What just happened? Athas asked in Theren's mind.

Before he could answer, Ial turned on her heel and left without another word, the doors slamming open before her as she did.

Ylia gave Theren one final look before following her mother.

Thank you, Theren said. She had just saved him.

Her regret and fear lingered in his mind as she left. Theren hushed his thoughts, nursing himself in the hollow space inside where no-one could reach him.

13

The minds of the Starspire were fluttering with excitement at the arrival of a new band of male visitors from far-flung spires. There was to be a Revel that evening, and Roshin was busy preparing some refreshments for the occasion. Valyn and Theren assisted her in mixing and pouring as required, faces dusted with the powders of cooking. The Growers might provide the essentials in abundance, but with additional tricks of heat, ice, and Light, the citizens of the spire made delicacies limited only by imagination.

"Why do only boys and girls get together at the Brotherwalk," Valyn enquired, wiping her cheek of the mixture she'd been stirring too enthusiastically.

"Because they're hoping to make children," Roshin replied, slicing vegetables at the bench.

"How?"

Though she tried to hide it, Roshin's discomfort was caught by both children.

"A child can only be made by a man and a woman when they come together in a particular way."

"Like when they kiss?" Valyn pressed on.

"That's part of it, but a kiss alone is not enough."

Theren stirred his bowl of batter quietly, watching the interaction between the two.

Valyn was quiet for a while, the sounds of cutting and mixing echoing around the kitchen.

"Can a girl kiss another girl?"

"Valyn!" Roshin's shock lashed in both children's minds, and Theren jumped. Valyn only glared.

"Don't ask such questions. If you're going to have such ideas" — Roshin tapped the side of her head — "keep them quiet. Best not to have them at all."

Though Theren's hands still trembled, he tried to put his mother out of his mind and focus. He could think of nothing save the word 'Dreamer' periodically ringing in his ears and the presence of the longing from his Dream.

Theren followed Athas, who led the way to the upper level of the Dreamers' Tower. The ascent was long; the constant pace up steps felt a more brutal drill than anything the Hunters had thrown at him. With a painful pang of sadness, Theren recalled the moment Hunter Feldan had called his name in The Choosing.

Athas led him through a crystal doorway where a huge room encircled the top of the tower — evidently some sort of dining and lounging space. Empty circular tables were strewn throughout the room along with low, broad chairs beside warmhearts and by the windows. Through elegant, open archways there was an expansive view of the spire and the forest, which glittered softly in the background. Night was falling, indicated by the slow dimming of the glass around them, the spire itself mimicking the descent of the sun. Theren yearned to be watching it from the edge of the forest, eyes set on the sky above.

He shook off the feeling and followed Athas to stand at an arched window. Several others in dark robes watched them silently, though Theren could feel their whispers to each other along the edges of his mind.

"There is much you wish to know," Athas began. "And I hardly know where to begin." They held each other's gaze a moment. "Perhaps, I can alleviate some of your worries first?"

Theren suppressed a sigh. He didn't know where to start either. He wondered if Valyn had been so restrained and felt his heart warm at the thought of her. At least she was not doomed to a Dreamer's life anymore.

"Why is this happening?" Theren asked finally.

Athas folded his hands within the billowing sleeves of his robe. "The simple answer is that this is happening because you are a Dreamer. Why is it happening now, and so late? I am hoping to understand myself."

"But I was tested as a boy," Theren protested. "By you." He let the implication hang; how did you miss it?

"Your mother made me test you after a nightmare. You were quite hysterical, she told me, and she feared it was a foretelling about her journey on the Speakerswalk." Athas' irritation flared. "Although I think her greater fear was the possibility you might be a Dreamer."

"But was it actually a foretelling?" Theren replied.

"I didn't think so at the time. I did not sense any Dreamer qualities in your sleep when we tested you. However..." Athas paused. "We never got a chance to prove it either way. Your mother missed the Speakerswalk that year."

Theren didn't need words to convey his shock.

"Yes," Athas continued. "Despite her dislike of us, she does listen to foretellings every now and then."

"But you said it wasn't one."

"Superstition gets the better of even the most sceptical of minds," Athas replied. "And now, I am beginning to think it was a foretelling and I missed it.

"How?" Theren's mind reeled.

"You are somehow..." Athas struggled to find the words "...apart from the rest of the spire. As though you are connected to us, but we are not connected to you."

Theren considered all of Roshin's, Valyn's, and Ylia's complaints over the years. He always thought his mind was just quieter than everyone else's.

"Your mind is blocked," Athas continued. "I almost can't sense anything you're feeling, except, I suspect, that which you choose to send out or when you feel a particularly strong emotion. Such as before." Athas sent a brief flash to him of their altercation with Ial only minutes ago. Theren could feel his terror through Athas' eyes.

"What does that have to do with Dreaming?" Theren asked, ignoring the discomfort of feeling his own emotion second-hand.

"I suspect you have an unconscious habit and have been blocking yourself, hiding away from the spire ever since you were a boy," Athas explained. "So, even asleep, I couldn't fully sense your experience. Who knows how many other Dreams you've had that we have missed." Athas shook his head.

"I never remember my dreams," Theren protested. "But I remember this one. And the one from when I was a boy..." Theren trailed off, trying to recall the details of that old dream. "I'm not sure whether I truly remember it, or if it was just talked about so much I *think* I do. I don't recall any others."

The sense of Athas' doubt alleviated somewhat, and he leaned against the crystal pillar of the arch, eyes sweeping across the room. Theren felt him send acknowledgement to several other Dreamers, who were keeping their distance, either clustered in small groups or sitting in chairs around several warmhearts spaced throughout.

"Well," Athas replied "It is an unsatisfying answer, but an answer all the same. Is there anything else you have a burning desire to ask?"

"What about this Dream?" Theren asked. "Do you know what it means?"

"No," Athas replied. Theren sent forth his disappointment and Athas sighed. "I'm disappointed too. Usually, I can tell the difference between a vision from the past and a foretelling, a warning or a simple message. This? It has the hallmarks of a foretelling, but I don't understand of what. There is no threat in the Dream. So perhaps it is something from the past?"

Theren gazed out into the glowing night. "It's something to do with the edge of the forest. After the Dream, I left the spire and —"

"You left the spire?" Athas cut him off. "At night? Alone?"

Theren sent a twinge of guilt, though it was mostly to appease his elder. The forests were his haunt; he was not afraid, and he did not regret his choice.

"Theren." Athas' voice was serious, and concern radiated from him so strongly, Theren felt the other Dreamers look over to them. "You cannot leave the spire after a Dream. You must not investigate."

"Why not?"

"What if it had been a threat?" Athas said. "You would have faced it alone."

"I can handle myself," Theren insisted sulkily.

"Remember what I said earlier?" Athas continued. "About the Dreamers' madness? Investigating it, obsessing over it, is a step down a path from which you cannot return. Once you have a Dream, you share it with us." Athas waved around the room. "As a collective, we hold it, decipher it, and share the meaning with the Speaker. She and the Council decide what to do."

"Why not the Dreamer?" Theren protested, feeling strangely defensive. "If Ena chose the Dreamer to receive the message, why can't they be the ones to decide what to do with it?"

Athas took a step closer. "It doesn't belong to you, Theren. You are just the vessel. It is of Ena, and we are all of Ena. We all have her Light running through our bodies." Theren hid his disagreement, but in the absence of acquiescence, Athas pressed on. "Theren, one of the main ways to avoid madness is to share the

Dream. To share yourself. We help each other attune to reality." Athas' impatience was sharp and tinged with regret. "There is so much to teach you. It is quicker with children."

Theren was not sure that, even as a child, he would be willing to share himself with the Dreamers. He had no interest in submitting his innermost thoughts to the scrutiny of strangers. He examined the faces around him, finding none familiar. The pang of loss hit him hard; were he among the Hunters, he would know all their faces. He would be with his friends.

Not eager to argue with the Dream Master on his first night in the tower, nor ready to accept the restrictions suddenly being placed on him, Theren changed the subject.

"You said Dreams can be of things from the past?"

"Yes, memories of things the Listeners have forgotten."

"The Listeners forget things?"

"More than you can imagine," Athas replied. "We are a shadow of what we once were." He sighed. "The Listeners recall an insignificant portion of the past, nothing that helps us replicate the glory of the old days. The Alvar defeated an entire race of monsters — what power we must have had. Do you think we could destroy an entire civilisation now?"

Theren sent him a mental shrug; who was he to know what it took to destroy the Void? No one even recalled what they looked like.

Athas' frustration simmered down.

"That is beside the point, I suppose. But we must understand whether your Dream is from the past or the future."

Theren felt the tug from the edge of the forest aching in his chest. It had felt so urgent at the time, but now it was only a faded pang.

"What if it is neither past, nor future?" Theren whispered.

Theren felt a sharp rebuke and jumped. He sensed the other Dreamers straining to overhear from behind him; the rebuke Athas had sent was not for him.

"Come," Athas said. "Let me show you to your room and settle you in for the night."

Athas indicated for Theren to follow, and the two of them strode from the room. Theren felt him summon someone. "Let me introduce you to Dreamer Leyen. He is not much older than you, and he will be helping you with your training."

His training. A loss lanced through Theren's chest once more. He was supposed to be with the Hunters, and his training was, largely, supposed to be over.

"Can I see Hunt Master Feldan?" Theren asked. "To explain?"

Athas paused at the top of the stair with a sigh.

"He knows, Theren," Athas explained, regret heavy in the air. "Everyone knows by now."

Theren followed Dreamer Athas downstairs. They walked in silence until they reached Valyn's — now Theren's — room. Waiting for them in the hall was a young man, perhaps only a few years older than Theren, of short stature and with pale yellow curls that sat at his chin.

It was an austere space, with little more than the essentials and no window. Some of Theren's belongings had already been delivered from his old room, laid out on the bench to the left of the door. Theren wondered at the presence of the two beds in the room. The young man behind them followed them in.

"Theren, this is Dreamer Leyen," Athas introduced them. "He will be staying with you at night. New Dreamers cannot sleep alone."

Dreamer Leyen sent him apologetic reassurance as Theren's stomach sank. He had no interest in having his mind watched while he slept.

"Could you share the Dream with me?" Dreamer Leyen asked.

"I already told the Dream Master about it," Theren replied.

"We need you to share it properly," Athas replied. "The version you gave me was...not entirely honest."

Theren repressed a flare of defensiveness. Did the Dreamers intend to invade his every privacy? He could not sleep alone, and now they wanted the Dream in detail. *His* Dream, as he had come to think of it. Even though it had crushed his hopes and diverted the course of his coming-of-age, he had come to feel a strange affinity with it.

"Alright," he said, and he sat down on the bed. Athas sat beside him, and Leyen settled on the spare bed alone. Theren took a deep breath and tried to relax, repeating the Dream in his mind's eye; from waking up, thinking he was in his room, to being compelled through the forest, standing at the tree line looking into nothing. He kept to the facts of the Dream, hiding away the parts of himself that felt the tug towards the forest. He finished on the symbol at the conclusion of the Dream.

"This is a sigil," Athas said. "It has to be."

Theren steered his mind away from illicit childhood memories. He shouldn't have known about the sigil. If he tried hard enough, he could almost believe he *didn't* know about the sigil.

"What does it mean?" Athas wondered aloud. Theren could feel his concentration as he tried to make sense of the story. "And there was no one else in your dream?"

Theren sent him his confirmation.

"Did you sense her?"

"Who?"

"Ena herself."

Athas held his gaze.

"I don't think so," Theren replied, questions blooming in his mind. The Speaker was the only one who could hear Ena, or so they were told.

Athas sent forth consternation. "You are not sharing the Dream properly with us, Theren. You need to let us in," he said, and he held out his hand. "Do it again, but properly this time. Hold nothing back."

Theren stared at Athas' outstretched hand. Were it someone like Valyn or Ylia requesting it, Theren wouldn't have needed to take it. But sharing a memory with someone when you did not have an affinity with them was easier with physical contact to anchor you to each other. Theren hesitated, not eager to have someone in his mind again after what his mother had just tried to do.

"What I said to the Speaker was not an exaggeration, Theren," Athas cautioned. "If we do not understand this and get it under control, you will lose touch with reality. You will slip into madness."

"What kind of madness?" Theren asked, stalling.

"You will become obsessed with your Dreams, which is bad enough when you have experienced only one, but imagine the effect of many. Some Dreamers start to act out their Dreams while they sleep. You may lose the ability to tell whether you are awake or not. You might even begin to hallucinate. It is frightening enough to watch, and I can't imagine what it is like to live through."

"Why does that happen? Why would Ena do that to us?" Theren asked.

"We do not fully understand Ena's will, Theren," Athas replied. "She is our Light itself; the very source of power in Starspire. It is not only us that can suffer from an Entity's gifts; the Light-mad ogyr you felled can attest to that. Power can corrupt all living beings. It follows that us mere mortals would not be able to manage her presence in our minds without strict protocols."

Theren swallowed. He did not want to go mad, but there were memories relevant to his Dream he didn't want Athas to know; his countless journeys to the edge of the forest as a child, his experiments with the sigil, the times he took Valyn out with him. It was reckless. Not the actions of the exemplary boy everyone thought he was. Not to mention, it would get Valyn in trouble, just like he had got her unfairly labelled as a Dreamer that morning.

"What if it's not really a proper Dream?" he asked. "How did you sense it in Valyn?" It did not matter that Athas had convinced him of the facts. He'd had his mind invaded once that day, and he was not eager for the sensation again.

Athas' twinge of impatience was quickly pushed aside as the Dream Master calmed himself. He rested his hands gently on his knees. Dreamer Leyen watched impassively.

"Theren, I fear I failed you all those years ago when your mother came to me and demanded you be tested early." Athas sent an apology heavy with regret. "This would all be easier if you had come to live with us as a boy. As would a lot of things, I am sure." He held Theren's gaze, meaning heavy between them. "Nonetheless, I need you to show me the Dream." He presented his hand again.

There was no choice. Theren cleared his mind of guilty memories, regrets, and fears, focusing on the beginning of the Dream. He took Athas' hand and closed his eyes, relaxing his mind to let the man in.

The sense of opening himself to Athas was nothing like when he and Valyn merged, nor the occasions when his mother mind-walked him. It was almost like nothing at all, except he found fragments of the dream resurfacing with no apparent pattern. He had a vision of himself waking, remembering the urge to investigate the edge of the forest. Though he did his best to hold some facts back, his emotions betrayed him while Athas had full access to his mind.

"You did recognise the sigil," Athas remarked at the end of the dream, releasing Theren's hand. "You can't lie to me, Theren."

Furious at being caught out, Theren closed himself off. Athas' brow furrowed ever so slightly.

"What?" Theren asked.

"You've gone again."

"Gone?"

"Blocked. I can only sense your absence, like there's a shadow here instead of you," Athas remarked. "Your mother and sister are the only ones I've ever known to be able to do that." He paused. "Roshin said you and Valyn fell asleep together?"

Theren hoped his embarrassment was hidden behind the alleged 'absence' Athas referred to.

"I know what that sounds like, but we are not —"

Athas sent forth his appeasement. "I can sense that there is nothing untoward between you." The Dream Master rubbed his temples and sighed. Weariness seeped from him. "But I know what has happened." Athas stood and made for the door. "The night of the Dream, you were merged with Valyn. I sensed the Dream through her mind since she is not blocked like you. But there is no doubt about it. It was your Dream, Theren."

Theren's heart sank. There truly was no going back. He was a Dreamer.

14

Theren no longer wore the amulet of infancy, but Valyn had not yet demonstrated sufficient control over her emotions. She was one of the last remaining who wore it. Her shame at the fact was suffocating when Theren curled up beside her at night. It didn't stop him from taking her hand, bypassing the amulet's power so they could fall asleep together.

But that night, Valyn pulled her hand away.

"What's wrong?"

"I don't want the Brotherwalk to come here when I'm grown up," Valyn murmured after a long period of silence.

Theren was quiet for a while. "I am scared to go on it," he said finally.

Valyn rolled back over to face him.

"I won't tell anyone," she promised.

"Fall asleep with me?" he asked.

She rested her wrist in his hand, and he wrapped his fingers around the amulet. As his sense of self lessened, he felt a lurking, black shame nagging at the back of his mind; not his, but no less strong. The face of a girl from Valyn's class flickered behind his eyes, intermingled with longing.

"I won't tell anyone," he whispered.

Though he did not know how he did it, he wiped the shame away. In its place, he held the memory of the edge of the forest, where the Hunters had taken the boys that day. He shared the wonder of the broken spire in the valley of the Abyss, and his questions about the Void.

He felt Valyn sigh and smile. Sleep came quickly with the view of an open field. The mysteries of the Void were far preferable than the mysteries of the heart.

Theren was dressed in his nightgown from home, feeling a little silly.

"So" — he looked at Dreamer Leyen — "are you going to watch me all night?"

Dreamer Leyen sat on the edge of the other bed, humour emanating from him.

"I will not be 'watching' you. I will be asleep too. But I will be able to sense if you Dream again."

Theren sighed and flopped down onto the bed. It was comfortable, but half the size of his opulent bed at home. He supposed he was going to give that up anyway, as he never intended to continue living in the luxury of the Speaker's Tower. Still, in that moment, he allowed himself to mope about yet another thing he'd lost.

He rolled over to face the crystal wall. Ena's glow was dim, and he reached out to place his hand on the glass.

Why me, Ena?" he asked to no one. Ena, of course, did not reply. The Entities did not converse. No, they sent strange dreams that no one understood and only communicated to the Speaker, regardless of her integrity.

Theren closed his eyes, wishing he could reach for Valyn, or Roshin. With Dreamer Leyen watching, he would be a fool to breach the Dreamers' rules. He would remain severed from the spire while he learned to control his gift. His curse.

His thoughts were a bitter lullaby that did a poor job of sending him to sleep. After some indiscernible time had passed, he gave up trying to sleep and opened his eyes. The room was near-dark. He stood and stretched, taking in

Dreamer Leyen's sleeping form breathing gently beside him. Like someone had thrown a hook through his stomach, he felt a pull urging him to the edge of the forest. Theren turned his head in the direction of the sigil at the forest's edge, like a wolf turning to the summoning of his pack. A vision of the edge of the forest filled the room, and it felt as though he was there in reality; standing on the tree line, staring into blank nothingness. A weight pushed against his chest and the symbol of the sigil flared in his face, bright and pale blue. For a moment, he could not tell whether he was in his room or at the forest's edge.

He squeezed his eyes shut, and when he opened them again, he was standing in the room in the Dreamers' Tower once more. Lest he waken Leyen, he hurried back to bed and pulled the covers over himself. Had he been Dreaming? Or was it just a memory? He didn't know.

Theren awoke the next morning and he sensed Leyen stir. Theren watched the kindly man, keeping his thoughts guarded even as he brushed the edges of Leyen's mind. Leyen felt tired, but there was no sense of anything amiss.

"Good morning," Theren said. Leyen returned the greeting. Theren waited.

"You didn't Dream last night?" Leyen asked. Theren could feel the man's confusion; he was fishing. Leyen couldn't tell either way.

"No," Theren replied – unsure whether his strange vision last night had been a Dream. "I told Dream Master Athas already. It seems I've only had the Dream once."

"That's not unusual," Leyen replied. "Most Dreams only come once, which is why we must be quick to record them in our collective memory." The young man sent forth waves of reassurance. No wonder Athas chose him for the new recruits. "Come." Leyen threw back his covers, still clad in a Dreamer robe. "Get ready for the day, and I will show you to breakfast. We will get you measured for your robes today too. Can't be Dreaming in a common nightgown!"

Leyen led Theren up the tower stairs to the uppermost landing, which housed the continuous room that ringed the tower. Along the inner wall were several tables of food, and the Dreamers were milling about in silence, collecting plates and bowls to break their fast. Some sat in groups around the warmhearts, others stood alone by the arched windows. In the light of a new day, Theren was able to admire the design of the arches decorated with finely worked glass to create a vine-like pattern along the edging. Theren spotted Dream Master Athas eating alone by an arch and, though Athas had not looked his way, Theren sensed the summons.

Theren ignored the breakfast table and joined him.

"You didn't have to come right away," Athas said as Theren sat in one of the crystal chairs. "You can get something to eat first."

"I'm not hungry," Theren replied truthfully. With time to think overnight his only appetite was for information. "You said something yesterday, when the Speaker was coming, about how the spire truly works. What did you mean?"

A twinge of regret emanated from Athas. "I spoke from arrogance," he replied. "The Speaker can commune with Ena in a way none of us can. But, even then, Ena's messages are vague, confusing. No Speaker could truly claim to comprehend an Entity's will. It is the same in all the spires across Alvaren. The messages an Entity sends through the Dreamers help build a picture of their intention."

Only the Speaker, and her daughter, knew what it was like to communicate with Ena. Theren realised he'd never even thought to ask Ylia about it.

"Sometimes," Athas continued, "I become frustrated at the Speaker's minimisation of our role in supporting her. But it was wrong of me to bring you into that. She's your mother."

Theren searched Athas' impassive face, wondering, for some reason, what the man's smile would look like. How many men's smiles were missed since they spent so little time with children? Only their lovers from other spires would see them, as facial expressions became important when communicating with those whose Light came from a different source.

"The Speaker is my mother in name alone," Theren replied, feeling an impassioned speech building about Roshin's role in raising him. He thought better of it; he was getting distracted.

Athas appeared content to let the topic drop. "I have a question for you now," the Dream Master said. "What happened between you and the Speaker yesterday? It felt...odd."

Theren pushed down the sick feeling in his stomach as he recalled his mother's mind in his. She had tried to mind-walk him; to take control of his consciousness. It was a forbidden act; a violation of the privilege of Ena's Light. Ena did not grant the people such power for them to use it against each other. The Alvar of each spire were connected, their Entities uniting them, a privileged experience of unity and differentiation. Though some were stronger in their use of Light, they should always serve the greater good. There was no good in forcing people to act against their will by dominating their minds.

But Theren had always wondered in a hidden corner of his mind what happened when their most powerful *did* violate the rules? What would happen if someone small spoke out against someone big. Surely nothing. Who would question the Speaker? And what could they do? No one matched her power. No, there would be no point in telling Athas the truth. It would simply make things harder. Now that he was a man, and with his seclusion in the Dreamers' Tower offering some protection, the past was the past.

"Nothing," Theren replied. "We just argued. A long-standing habit." He sensed Athas didn't believe him but was grateful when he chose to let it drop. Theren changed the subject.

"Another thing I don't understand," Theren said, pausing to feel Athas confirm he was listening. "I truly do not recall my dreams. I only somewhat remember the one when I was a child, and this recent one. Surely two such dreams are not enough to qualify me as a Dreamer?"

Athas leaned back in the chair and crossed a leg over the other.

"You are correct; a dream alone does not make you a Dreamer. You have the blessing but now you need the skill. I expect with training, and undoing that mental barrier you've raised, you will begin to recall your dreams and be more open to Ena's messages. Perhaps she has been trying to reach you all these years and you were cut off. I do not know, but together we will find out."

Theren recalled Athas' words yesterday. He would need to share his mind properly with the others. The denizens of the spire were used to being connected, though Theren knew now he had always held himself apart. He had done so unintentionally, but now he wasn't so sure he was ready to give it up.

"How do I do that? Undo a barrier I didn't even know I had raised?"

Athas leaned forward. "There is much to teach you, and it won't be learnt over breakfast. But, broadly speaking, there are two fundamental skills you must master. First, is the ability to Dream-walk. The second is to Tether." Theren waited for further explanation. "There are several steps to master these skills," Athas continued. "But the first and most important of both abilities is to be able to tell if you are awake or asleep."

"Well, that's easy," Theren replied. "I'm awake now."

Athas' mirth was gentle. "Is that so? How do you know?"

Theren held his tongue as his mind went blank. How did he know? What if this was a Dream? A nightmare in which he lost his Hunter status and would never see his friends again? He sent his uncertainty to Athas as his gaze dropped to the floor.

"It's alright," Athas reassured him. "You are awake, and knowing that is the easy part."

Theren pushed aside a seed of doubt; his Dream had felt real while he was having it. It was only after he'd awoken that he could tell what it had been. Who was to say if this moment was any different?

"More critically," Athas continued, oblivious to Theren's turmoil, "what we need for you to be able to do is be aware when you're asleep and *remain* asleep. When you can do that, we are at the beginning of your ability to Dream-walk."

"What is -"

"Patience." Athas lifted a hand, and Theren snapped his mouth shut. "The second ability is to be able to Tether. To ensure we remain in touch with reality, that we don't lose ourselves to Dreams, all Dreamers must Tether themselves to each other. It is not dissimilar to the connection we all share within the spire, but enhanced. I am constantly able to check whether I am of sound mind through my link to the Tether; the collective consciousness of all the other Dreamers who provide a baseline for sanity."

"How much of yourself do you have to reveal to Tether?" Theren swallowed, feeling a rising fear in his throat.

Athas' presence was serious. "All of you, Theren. How can we know what is normal if we are not all honest? Every urge, every shame, every desire. All the experiences of being alive."

Theren sent him a curt acknowledgement, but felt the urge to run quiver through his legs. No wonder the Dreamers took their protégés as children. It would be far easier to Tether a child; children had little privacy as their minds were undisciplined and they had not experienced a lifetime of mistakes and secrets to keep. Theren had plenty of those, and not only his, but secrets he kept for others as well; Valyn's hidden desires, his and Ylia's memories of their mother. The Dreamers wanted to know his mind in a way no one else had.

Regret lanced through him. He had kept so much of himself separate, even from the people he loved most. Roshin, Valyn, Ylia, each of them would have had all of him, and loved every part, and he didn't even let himself truly connect with them. Now he was going to have to give himself over to strangers.

If only he could leave the Tower to prepare for the Revel and the Brotherwalk — even if he had been afraid of it. He would do anything to return to the way things were. What he wouldn't give to take a sprint through the forest or track with the Hunters.

The longing in his chest altered, making room for an urgency that pulsed through his body. He lifted his head to look out the arched window to the forest. No, it was not the Hunt he yearned for. He wanted to leave the Tower to check the sigil again, to sit at the edge of the forest. There, he could forget all this and just watch the sky turn from day to night in a way the spire could never satisfy.

"I really can't leave the Dreamers' Tower at all, can I?" Theren murmured. Athas sent his surprise at the change of subject.

"No, not yet. Just for a few weeks, while we get you Tethered. It won't be forever."

"I can't even visit Ylia, or Valyn?"

Athas was apologetic. "No, Theren. Not for now."

"Why?" Theren asked, exasperated. "Why can't I go out during the day and return at night?"

He sensed distrust from Athas and wondered whether the man meant to send it.

"Not until I'm satisfied with your training. It is better to be safe than sorry."

Theren bit back further argument and sent forth his resignation. He ignored the tug coming from the edge of the forest. He needed to focus. If he was a Dreamer now, best learn how to control it. Ena had handed him a long-knife, and he'd be a fool to swing it blindly.

"Well." He looked at Athas. "Let's start training then."

15

Theren retracted the bow and held the tension with all his might, his arm trembling with the effort. His muscles protested with the strain, begging him to release the bowstring, but he refused to waver.

He was going to be a Hunter one day, and he'd prove it.

Hold, the Hunt Master said in their minds. Theren felt the struggles of the other boys, half wishing they could give up, the other half as determined as he. He closed his eyes and ignored the strain on his fingers and his arm. He flared his Light to help him.

No Light, the Hunt Master reminded firmly. Theren drew on every ounce of inner strength he had; every stubborn urge he'd ever ignored — delved deep into the helpless fury he felt every time his mother won an argument or mind-walked him away.

The twang of several arrows being released nearly caused him to open his eyes, but he didn't need sight to know what had happened. From the despair of the other boys, he knew they had failed. Several others lowered their bows.

Hold, Theren. *The Hunt Master's voice was encouraging. Theren felt his thrill of anticipation; the challenge implied. How far could Theren be pushed?*

Resolve strengthened, Theren cleared his mind. He wiped the pain away and became little more than a shell of quivering muscles. Time didn't matter. He was strong, even without the aid of his Light.

"Release," Hunt Master Feldan's voice was like an eagle's cry. Theren opened his eyes, his aim still true, and loosed the arrow. The agony of his muscles finally releasing thundered through him, his fingers numb. The arrow stuck in the target with a resounding thud. Not a bullseye, but a hit all the same.

Feldan didn't need to say anything. The approval was clear. Theren allowed himself a small flicker of satisfaction as the other boys congratulated him.

Training with the Hunters had been thrilling and fun; nothing reminded one of the privilege of being alive so well than facing down a Light-mad monster. In contrast, training with the

Dreamers was a frustrating exercise in tedium and stillness. Theren sat, eyes closed, in a large hall. Athas was beside him.

"You are not focused, Theren," Athas spoke aloud, and Theren pulled his thoughts away from fond memories of training with the Hunters as a boy.

For the past few days, Theren had been forced to sit in silent meditation. Athas had taken the lead in his training, sitting quietly with him, and attempting to coax Theren's mind into relaxing. Aside from abject boredom, Theren didn't feel any different.

"Sorry," Theren replied, opening his eyes. His posture slumped. He was tired of this.

He looked around the large room the Dreamers called the Hall of Echoes. It was windowless and curved like most architecture in the spire. Amidst the vaulted ceiling were several shining orbs that drifted overhead, casting shimmers around the room like water catching light. The walls were so covered with sigils that the very air felt energised, as though a lightning storm had been contained within. Athas explained the design of the hall enhanced the memories of Dreams so the Dreamers could study them collectively. It kept a pure version of a Dream, unaltered by the judgements and memories of the Dreamers as they recalled it.

In here, the sigils that distanced the minds of the Dreamers from the rest of the spire were plentiful; studying Dreams required concentration and seclusion. Though Theren had been able to muster a vague sense of Valyn and Roshin while in the rest of the Tower, in here, he had no sense of the outside world at all. Athas and the others assured him that it was all with the intention of protecting the Dreamers and the spire.

He remembered the feeling of his mother reaching into Athas' mind the day he arrived, despite the sigils, and wondered if she could get in here. Perhaps this was the safest place in the spire, though the thought was tinged with bitterness. Safe from his mother he may be, but a deep ache had settled in his chest at being separated from his friends, especially from Ylia and Elsie. Try as he might to accept his fate as a late Dreamer, the resentment burned like a coal within. He was lonely and frustrated.

"Perhaps a break," a voice spoke behind him. He turned to see Dreamer Talith, another who had been recruited to train him, standing beside his nocturnal guard, Dreamer Leyen. Under better circumstances, Theren thought he would have liked both Leyen and Talith, but things as they were, all the kindly efforts of his teachers felt like inescapable pressure.

Not in the least because the first task in order to Tether was to release his mental blocks. A task for which Theren had neither the ability nor motivation. The prospect of all his fears and desires being laid bare for the Dreamers to know filled him with cold dread, let alone the thought of revealing his secrets. Secrets like the way the sigil from the Dream floated behind his eyes as he fell asleep at night, and the way his chest constantly felt pressure bearing down upon it with the desire to escape. Theren turned his head and wished for a window to look out.

"The sigil in my dream," Theren murmured. "Have you discussed that with the other Dreamers. With the Council?"

Athas' disapproval was gentle. "You do not need to worry about that, Theren. It is important that the Dreamer stay separate from the discussions about the Dream beyond the tower, especially when you are new."

Theren released a flare of irritation. "Sir, I don't mean disrespect, but that seems foolish to me."

Athas had the grace to respond with humour. "Oh? And tell me what you know about how all this works?"

"It just doesn't seem wise to exclude the person with the best knowledge of the Dream," Theren replied, sending forth humility.

"You shared the Dream with me," Athas replied. "I know it as well as you. We have relived it in the Hall of Echoes and examined it many times. I felt the same pull you felt; I saw the symbol. I could draw it from memory. In fact..."

Athas drew the sigil in the air with his Light where it hovered for a moment before evaporating. Theren confirmed it was correct, still unsatisfied at his exclusion. Athas watched him for a moment.

"Theren, have you ever had a friend come to you with a problem and ask for your advice to solve it?"

"Of course."

"They share their memory of the argument, or their thoughts on their position," Athas continued. "And yet, though you fully understand their struggle, you can offer a new perspective. Objectivity."

"It's not the same," Theren protested.

"Isn't it?" Athas replied gently. "Right now, you want to tell me I'm not taking the Dream seriously enough, despite there being no recurrence of the Dream and no indication that it's a foretelling."

"I feel that it's serious," Theren said. Athas lifted a hand to stop him before he went on.

"You feel it as strongly as a friend might feel they are right about something, even when you know they are not."

Theren fought off a frown, the childish urge surprising him. What was wrong with him? He was a man now, well, as close as one could be without going on the Brotherwalk. Being trapped in this tower and treated like a fool was making him regress.

He needed Roshin's wisdom to set him straight. He could try to push past the sigils that kept the Dreamers hidden. It might take a bit of Light to do so, but if Ial could get in, surely he could reach out?

"You're right, Dreamer Talith," Athas said suddenly. "A break for today is warranted. Come, Theren, let's get something to eat."

Athas stood and offered Theren his hand. Theren felt a stab of mistrust; what if Athas intended to use the physical contact to invade his mind? He scolded himself. Athas wouldn't do that.

He took the man's hand, who helped him to his feet.

"I've got a desire for redfruit tisane," Athas declared, sweeping from the room. Theren followed, the seed of suspicion growing roots in his gut.

After a short break, they returned to training. Theren sat down once again in the centre of the Hall of Echoes; Athas sat in front of him. Theren prepared to relax his mind and try to enter the meditative state that Athas had been attempting to instil in him.

"Perhaps we could work on Dream-walking instead?" Leyen suggested.

Theren felt Athas consider the suggestion.

"It is not wise until he is Tethered," Dreamer Talith replied, leaning against the door. Her long, silver hair was tossed over her shoulder in a loose braid, her sharp eyes watching them.

"Let us show you a Dream then," Athas suggested. "And the first stage of Dreamwalking."

He got to his feet and Theren followed suit. The Dream Master waved his hand and the room became dark.

"You're about to experience an old Dream," Athas said. "Don't fear — none of it can hurt you."

Theren straightened his back.

In a flash, images in three dimensions appeared around him, pale in the silver-blue light of Ena. He caught a glimpse of a giant stag running along a forest floor, the trees spinning past them as though they, too, were racing with the creature. Theren stumbled, dizzy. He had a sense of fear, urgency, anticipation. An arrow shot past him, and he dodged, flaring his Light reflexively to alter the air currents around him. With the swirl of colour all around him, he lost his sense of where he was in space. His dodge quickly turned into a fall, and he landed on his behind with a sharp shock. Before he could make any sense of what he was seeing, it was over.

Theren breathed heavily, and he blinked several times to orient himself.

"Dreams are intense, aren't they?" Athas asked rhetorically, with a hint of mirth. He pulled Theren to his feet.

"What does it mean?" Theren panted.

"That's not important yet," Athas replied. "What's important is that you need to be able to move freely through the Dream, control it in a sense, in order to study it."

"It is easier to understand Dreams once you are Tethered," Talith added. "Because you share the collective knowledge of all of us. You know what to look for, what patterns from Ena stand out."

"Use your Light to slow it down first," Athas instructed. "Dreams do strange things with time. They do not last very long, but to the Dreamer, they can feel timeless, unbound. In the case of Dreamers madness, they don't seem to end," he added.

Before Theren could reply, Athas waved his hand and called up the Dream again. This time, Theren fixed his focus on the stag, using his Light to try to control the moving pieces of the Dream. Though he found himself feeling less disoriented, he made no impact on the flow of the Dream."

"Well, at least you didn't fall over that time," Talith said, amused.

"At this rate," Theren grumbled, examining the ithlyn on his hands, "I am going to have no Light left in me after this training."

"Again," Athas said, ignoring the complaint.

Theren braced himself, determined to succeed. He had felled an ogyr. He would not let some figures in Light best him.

That evening, after making frustratingly little progress in training, Leyen tried to make him feel better by properly introducing Theren to some other Dreamers, young and old alike. The tower was not crowded; Ena's gift was selective. As Leyen explained, at most it appeared in only one or two people each year. When Theren asked Leyen in front of the others how many of them ended up mad in the end, the feeling of awkward anxiety became almost unbearable. Theren never got his answer.

By the time he returned to his room after picking listlessly at dinner, Theren's frustration had boiled into the air. He'd not seen Athas again, the other Dreamers had shunned him, and Leyen's infuriating pleasantness had not wavered.

Despite knowing more about the Dreamers' ways and commencing training, Theren felt more adrift than when he'd first arrived. He felt his outsider status keenly; a late Dreamer unable to connect with the others. He would be forced to submit his mind to a collective of esoteric 'expert sleepers' as Valyn would have called them, and every Dream he was gifted would be shared and dissected without him too. Perhaps, worst of all, his Dreams would be shared with his mother, who would have the ultimate say over what to do about it. He was simply a messenger. A vessel. Nothing of value; simply a part of the whole.

As Theren lay in bed, hoping Leyen was asleep, he decided he'd had enough of his roiling thoughts. He needed a familiar voice in his head, not these well-meaning — but strange — Dreamers. He hushed his mind, sloughed off his uncertainty, and stole from the room. He used his Light to form a cushion of air around his bare feet, hiding the soft slap of his footsteps on the crystal floors as he ran up the stairs. His midnight-blue robes billowed silently around him.

The sigils on the walls of the tower glistened in the dim glow of the tower; the same sigils that made his excursion necessary. If he could just talk to someone outside, he wouldn't need to sneak about.

He was panting by the time he reached the top of the tower, but he did not stop to rest. He hurried to the open windows. There, the arches framed the view over the dimmed city below, but Theren wasted no time taking it in. Instead, he tucked and tied up his Dreamer's robe to give his legs better movement and launched himself up to top of the arch. The sculpted glass offered multiple handholds for climbing, but the dome above the arches was smooth and lacked purchase. Theren was forced to flare his Light and boost himself up, almost weightless for a moment, to get out onto the dome. Up there, he used his Light to adhere his hands and feet to the glass until he found a place to sit safely. As he settled in, he examined the ithlyn on his hands, hoping their faded glow would not be too noticeable to the others. He had just used a lot of Light.

He looked out across the spire, the pull from the edge of the forest nagging at him still. He could just leave altogether and check the sigil. With a glance at his robes and bare feet, he realised that would surely end badly. He dismissed the thought and focused on what he came here to do. He cast his mind out, relishing the familiar hum of thousands of minds beneath him. How silent these past few days had felt.

Ylia?

Though he ached to check on Valyn or seek out Roshin's wisdom, the person he needed to talk to the most was his sister. As Apprentice Speaker, she would be sitting on the Council and would no doubt hear about his Dream soon, if she had not already.

Ylia was asleep but awakened with a start. Theren felt several emotions flit across her mind before she controlled her thoughts and hushed her shock and confusion.

Theren? Where are you?

Theren sent her the impression of where he was sitting, on the dome above the Dreamers' Tower with the spire glistening at his feet. He glanced up to the Speaker's Tower, where somewhere within his sister lay abed.

What are you doing up there? she scolded.

Has the Council met about my Dream yet?

Exasperation flowed from her. *We're meeting today, but your Dream is just one item on the agenda.*

You're not so important that a whole meeting would be called about you.

Theren bristled. *I'm not important, but the Dream is.*

Is it a foretelling?

I don't know.

A memory?

No, I don't think so.

Irritation came from her again. *Well, it's either one or the other. Past or future.*

Theren pushed his frustration back against her. He wasn't here for a lecture.

I don't think Athas is taking it seriously.

Ylia's annoyance shifted towards concern. *The Dreamers don't know you're out of the tower, do they?* Theren took care to hide his guilt. *Have you been feeling alright?*

Theren didn't hide his anger. How convenient it was to ascribe madness to a Dreamer when you didn't want to hear what they had to say.

I'm perfectly fine.

He felt Ylia press against his mind. *Prove it.*

Theren held himself closer. *What do you know about Dreaming madness? Besides, someone might overhear.*

The excuse was poor; the two children of the Speaker were powerful enough to escape notice. An expectant silence greeted him. Theren sighed and relaxed his mind slightly. His sense of his sister grew stronger until he almost felt as though she were sitting right beside him. He felt some tension leave him; how he'd missed her, waking up to her breakfasts and banter.

How's Elsie? he asked. In response, an impression of his niece shimmered behind his eyes, the little girl practising drawing with Light in the air. *You're letting her use Light already?* Elsie was little more than a toddler, nowhere near ready to join minds with the spire.

She is powerful and clever, Ylia replied. *Unlike you, who is just the former.*

I'm clever enough.

You're an idiot, sneaking out of the tower like that. The Dreamers are separate for good reason. But at least you don't seem insane. He sensed her gentle presence in his mind still, turning over the emotions he felt. *We haven't discussed a Dream at Council for a while,* she said finally. Whether she meant to send the thought or not, Theren felt her worry.

What's wrong?

Are you sure you're alright? Nothing bad happened in the Dream?

No, nothing bad. Athas will share it with you tomorrow. But I don't think he will take it seriously enough. It's something to do with a lost sigil. We should send a Listener out to look at it, and maybe the Hunters to scout the tree line.

Ylia was hesitant.

Considering nothing bad happened in the dream, you feel... The word 'obsessed' flickered past, but she opted for another word. *Preoccupied.*

I'm fine! Theren dulled his frustration. *I'm fine, I promise.*

With reluctance, Ylia accepted his words. *Alright. I will suggest what you said. But the Hunters are busy scouting the forest in preparation for the Brotherwalk. I don't know if they'll spare anyone. You're hard to sense when you're in the Dreamers' Tower, but we meet at noon. I'll try to reach you tomorrow night to tell you how it went.*

Thank you, Ylia. Theren sent her the weight of gratitude that sat in his chest.

They said their goodbyes and Theren hurried down from the dome and into the tower before anyone was the wiser.

16

It was hard to lie in the spire. If you were powerful, you could get away with it. Children rarely did.

"I will ask one more time," the Hunter said, eying off the group with a frown. "Where are the long-knives?"

It was not Hunt Master Feldan teaching them that day, for which Theren was grateful. He wouldn't have liked lying to Feldan, and he wasn't even sure he could. The man was powerful.

Two long-knives had gone missing overnight, and no-one knew anything. The Hunter stalked along the line of boys, his presence bearing down on them one at a time. Theren felt the other boys shudder with the force of it. He stopped and grabbed the wrist of a late-blooming child who still wore the amulet of infancy. Theren didn't need to be connected to the boy to know *his fear; it was plain on his face. After a moment, the Hunter dropped the boy's wrist and moved to the next boy, then the next.*

He finally reached Theren. Theren held the man's gaze, saw the furrowed brow, felt the anger, and simply disappeared within himself. The Hunter was not the first angry adult to bear down on him, and he certainly wasn't the most frightening.

With a huff, the man moved on to the next boy.

A good thing, for stashed in the hollow of a tree, far above the city, were two long-knives, the location of which was known only by two souls. Theren and Valyn.

And, of course, no one would think to ask the girls.

"Theren!"

Theren's reverie was cut short by the sound of Talith's voice, a sharp rebuke forcing itself into his mind. He stood amidst a vision of Light; the retelling of another Dream. Movement swirled around him as figures danced in a circle, hands intertwined, men and women alike.

Sorry, he replied in her mind. Leyen stood at the door, observing, and Theren could feel his pity.

Talith waved her hand and the vision surrounding him disappeared. She sent forth her impatience.

"You're not paying attention," Talith accused. Theren lowered his gaze. She was right, of course. He had been caught in a memory. It had felt so real, almost as if he had been a child again, worrying about being caught in a lie.

He felt something pass between Talith and Leyen, but he didn't try to overhear. Athas was not there, of course. The Council was about to meet and he had more important things to do.

Like discussing Theren's Dream.

Anger bubbled in his gut. He should be the one to share it if he chose. He knew it best. It was his.

"Are you feeling well?" Leyen asked him. Theren seized his chance.

"Actually," Theren replied, fabricating a sense of exhaustion, "No, I don't."

Another exchange flickered between Leyen and Talith.

"You do feel weaker today," Leyen said. "We have been pushing him, Dreamer Talith. Athas has —"

Leyen was suddenly silent, no doubt due to a private rebuke from Talith.

"I do feel weak." Theren stooped and rested his hands on his knees, standing in the centre of the Hall of Echoes. He lowered his head and sighed. "This whole week — everything that has happened — being denied the Brotherwalk..."

Sympathy came from Leyen, nothing from Talith. Theren repressed his satisfaction.

"Have I been sleeping well, Leyen?" Theren asked quietly. He remembered the moments of shame and uncertainty Valyn had shared with him over the years and borrowed the feeling, the emotional cadence swirling around him. His heart almost broke, remembering Valyn's face, but he took care to bury that emotion deep.

"Perhaps a day of rest and contemplation is in order," Talith said. "Stay in your room, Theren." She turned to Leyen. "And you, watch over him. We will reconvene with Athas' help tomorrow."

It didn't takelong for Theren to shake Leyen. He spun a story about shame and disappointment and how he wanted an afternoon alone to practise everything Athas and Talith had been trying to teach him, free from judging eyes.

"Talith said I wasn't to leave you." Leyen hesitated as they alighted on the landing of Theren's room. It was past noon now, and

Theren's impatience gnawed at him. He needed to be alone, and Leyen's incessant pestering was going to thwart his plans.

What was the council saying about his Dream?

Theren reached into the young man's mind, feeling his weak conviction. He didn't really want to watch Theren all afternoon; he had the Brotherwalk to prepare for after all. Hopeful, Theren dug deeper. Leyen's mind lay before him. The young man felt sorry for him. As a boy, Leyen himself had been slow to learn, and his gift had come later in childhood. He knew well Theren's frustration and the shame of being slow at his lessons. Though it was something of an act in Theren, for Leyen it was a wound only freshly healed.

A freshly healed wound is easily reopened.

"You're right," Theren said aloud. "I'm sorry for even asking you."

Gently, hidden, Theren nudged the insecurities in Leyen's mind. How Leyen would have loved reprieve from the public failures he had suffered. Theren enhanced those memories, bringing them to the fore, heightening his emotion. He felt Leyen's heart sink and pressed deeper. How nice it would have been if someone had given

Leyen a rest; a chance to hide from the judging eyes of others. Who, now, was Leyen to deny a boy — a young man who had been denied his Brotherwalk and freedom — a moment of privacy? Theren had lost so much, after all.

"I suppose a few hours won't hurt," Leyen conceded as they stopped at Theren's door.

"It's alright, Leyen," Theren replied. He withdrew from the young man's mind, knowing Leyen's mind was changed.

"No." Leyen rested a gentle hand on Theren's shoulder. "It is hard to become a Dreamer, hard enough as a child, I can't imagine how hard it is for you now."

Theren offered a dry agreement. "The fact you can't imagine it means I'm obviously still failing at Tethering."

Leyen humoured him with a small laugh. "Take a few hours to yourself, Theren. I don't blame you for wanting them. I will come and check on you in a while."

Theren made sure to send him humble gratitude, and Leyen returned a flash of sympathy before he closed the door, leaving Theren to stare at the sigils on the glass walls of his room. A slimy, dark feeling grew in his stomach.

What he'd done to Leyen was not mind-walking, he told himself. It wasn't the same. And besides, it was for a purpose.

Dismissing his guilt, Theren sat on his bed and closed his eyes. When Valyn had been trapped in here, he had been able to sense her barest presence. The sigils might separate the minds of the Dreamers somewhat, but he had already seen that they could be overcome. Ial had forced her way into Athas' mind, and surely Athas communicated with the council freely from his room in the tower. Theren opened his mind, reaching out for the familiar feel of his sister. He could sense her, just, but she was hazy. He probed through the haze, like he was stumbling with his hands out through a fog. The sigils were effective.

Sometimes, sheer force was needed to achieve what finesse could not. Impatient, he flared his Light, not caring about the consequences, and reached out to Ylia. The familiar feel of her mind was a relief, and he pulled himself toward her. It was still wrong, murky, but he could see and feel more.

Several voices sounded in his ears and a blurry impression of the Speaker's council room formed in his mind. It was though he were viewing it underwater; he could make out the glass table and the chairs set around it, each filled with a shadowy figure he couldn't quite grasp. The person he sensed most strongly was his mother; her fury was poorly contained and burned through the room. Theren realised it was particularly amplified at Ylia. Theren's curiosity piqued.

Then came Ylia's sharp rebuke and the room disappeared.

Please, Theren begged. He gripped the tenuous connection between them tightly. He felt it strengthen. Ylia held him closer, and he found himself exhaling when he suddenly didn't need to expend so much effort. Though she allowed him to stay, she was not pleased to have him there. Her irritation was like a buzzing swarm of bees. He could feel the effort she was putting into maintaining contact with him.

Athas has told us about the Dream, Ylia explained. *He suspects it is a memory of the past. Everyone has agreed it requires no urgent action.*

He's wrong, Theren protested. Ylia firmly told him to shut up.

He heard Hunt Master Feldan speak and could not hide from his sister the longing that shot through him. Ylia's irritation with him softened.

"Are you sure Theren even is a Dreamer?" Feldan asked. "It seems strange that Ena would send him a non-urgent Dream so late in life."

Ial's voice cut through the room. "There is a chance you are wrong, and this is all nothing," the Speaker said to Athas.

"You have ruined the future of one of the most promising young men I've known," Feldan pressed on. "I've been wanting to discuss Theren's exclusion from the Brotherwalk. It isn't fair."

The Head Builder grumbled an agreement. Theren allowed himself to hope that, just perhaps, the pressure from the Council would be enough to let him leave the tower, for the Brotherwalk at least.

"Need I remind you of the tales?" Athas said, reprimand heavy behind his words. "You would risk the next version of the Mad Dreamer including the name of Starspire and Speaker Ial with it?"

Ial's venom was interrupted by the Head Grower.

"With no offence to you, Speaker Ial, the Dream Master is right..."

They argued back and forth about Theren's future and the validity of his Dreamer status for several minutes. Ylia didn't participate, and no one sought her views. Athas put an end to it with a force Theren didn't think was possible from the unassuming man.

"Enough! It is not open for debate. I do not dictate to the Builders how to craft a home, nor you, Feldan, on how best to fell an ogyr — though on the latter front you know I could."

A sense of disgruntled acceptance settled among the Council; Feldan and Ial were particularly displeased.

Tell them I think it's a warning. Something to do with the sigil, Theren urged Ylia.

Shut. Up.

"This sigil," Ylia spoke aloud. "Can you draw it for us, Dream Master?"

Theren sensed everyone's surprise and surmised that Ylia must not usually speak up at these meetings. Nonetheless, Athas waved his finger in the air and drew the sigil from the edge of the forest.

"You do not recognise it?" Ylia asked the Head Listener.

"It is unusual for a sigil to be found outside a spire," the Head Listener remarked. "I will ask our Listener brothers to inquire with the other spires as to whether they've heard of this phenomenon when they're on the Brotherwalk."

"Should we not study it?" Ylia asked.

"We will," the Head Listener replied. "But I do not relish the thought of sending my people to the edge of the forest with no escort. With all the able men about to leave on the Brotherwalk, there will be no one to take us, and fewer of us to study it."

Though Valyn's reasons for wishing to be a Hunter were self-serving, Theren couldn't help but think she was right to question tradition; having only men in charge of hunting and safeguarding the spire from the forest was folly, as times like this demonstrated.

Ylia's flare of irritation reminded Theren that now was not the time for such thoughts.

"There is no need to hurry," Athas reassured. "The sigil has been there for centuries. It's not going anywhere."

"And perhaps that's why the Dream didn't quite feel like a memory or a foretelling," Ylia added, though Theren could feel the comment was directed at him. "It was Ena making us aware of the sigil —"

"Yes! And perhaps communicating its function," the Head Listener interrupted, her excitement peculiar to that of a scholar who has solved a puzzle.

Ial turned her focus to Athas. "Is there any chance then that this is not a true Dream? That Theren has somehow picked up a message from Ena about the sigil?"

"There is no way for anyone to receive a message from Ena but through a Dream, or through you, Speaker. I think this particular Dream came through Theren because he already knew of the sigil," Athas explained. "He found it as a lad but never told anyone because he was aware he'd get in trouble for leaving the spire."

"Idiot boy," Ial hissed.

"Anyway," Ylia interjected. "It seems decided. This was an unusual Dream, in both its content and arrival, but a Dream nonetheless. Theren is a Dreamer and cannot partake in the Brotherwalk, sad though that is. The sigil will be investigated when enough of our brothers have returned from the Brotherwalk to guard the Listeners in the forest."

But that will be months from now! Theren protested.

In an instant, he was catapulted from Ylia's mind, briefly feeling the sensation of falling before he properly became aware of his body once more. She left him with a sense of impatience. He had pushed too far; sitting in her mind to listen to the council was one thing but bothering her while she was trying to listen and hold him with her all at once was another.

Theren slumped backwards on the bed and stared at the ceiling. He waved his hand above his face, noting the significant depletion of his Light. The dullness of his ithlyn was undeniable now.

What was wrong with him? The Speaker's Council had decided The Dream was nothing more than Ena helping the Listeners build their picture of history. An old sigil was an interesting tidbit about the past. It might have some utility now, but nothing so urgent it couldn't wait until after the Brotherwalk. Perhaps it was a sigil like Valyn had suggested; a way to ward off threats. That would explain its placement at the edge of the forest, facing that ruined spire in the field that surely belonged to the Void.

He could not explain why, but it didn't feel right. Something in him knew the Dream was more than that. He did not sense fear from the Dream, as he had as a boy when he'd Dreamt about his mother's Speakerswalk. Why, if it was nothing more than a memory of the past, did he find himself lost in memories of the forest's edge, imagining the sigil as he fell asleep each night? Why did he feel the pull towards the Abyss? He had always loved running through the forest but his yearning for the tangled tracks of branch and vine was something deeper. Something urgent. Being deprived his freedom was driving him mad.

He replayed Athas' words of caution from the other night. There are few good conclusions to the madness of an unchecked Dreamer. Was that happening to him?

"No," he said aloud to himself. "It is normal that locking me up would make me long for what I cannot have."

His freedom had been curbed, his hopes dashed, his access to those he loved severed.

He glanced at his hands again. He probably had enough Light for one more push. There was a good chance he would need a better excuse than the one he'd planned for why he had expended so much Light. He closed his eyes and felt for Valyn. A hazy sense of her formed in his mind and his heart warmed at her presence. He felt her recognise him.

He flared his Light to push past the sigils and grasped at the edges of her mind. The Light ran through him, weakening fast.

Valyn, he whispered. *If they ask, I was talking to you. Not Ylia.*

The last thing he felt was Valyn's concerned confusion before blackness consumed him.

17

Theren couldn't sense Ylia anywhere. He searched her room, high and low, and still nothing. Of course, it would be hard to find her; she was wearing his amulet.

He felt a glimmer of her presence from somewhere behind him at the same time as he heard her voice call his name from all directions. In a heartbeat, she was gone again.

A thrill of excitement ran through him, but he did his best to control it. He wasn't supposed to have his amulet off yet. But Ylia insisted that hide and seek was more fun when she could communicate with him. It meant she could hide in harder places.

He advanced on the large chest near her door and heard a sudden creak behind him. With a flash of Light and the soft sounds of footsteps, he knew she had moved spots.

"That's cheating!" he lamented, anger bubbling up alongside joy and anticipation. The feelings were bold and colourful and made him laugh aloud, giddy with excitement. It always took so long to find her, but it was so satisfying when he finally did. "I'm going to find you!" he shouted, half-giggling.

His giggles died when the force of rebuke filled his mind so strongly that he fell to his knees.

What are you doing? His mother's voice obliterated his own thoughts. You're being so loud! Just about everyone in the tower can hear you!

"Theren?" Ylia's voice came from somewhere. "What's wrong?"

Why is your amulet off? came his mother's furious question. He sensed her moving through the tower towards them.

"Oh no," he heard Ylia groan as he felt her trepidation. In a moment she was beside him, tying the amulet onto his wrist. As soon as the stone hit his skin, it was like he had stepped into a vacuum. No hum of minds, no fury from his mother. Just sweet silence.

Ial burst through the door a moment later.

There was no explanation aloud. By the frightened look on Ylia's face, a conversation was happening between her and their mother that Theren couldn't hear.

Ial turned her focus on Theren, grabbing his wrist and covering the amulet. The force of her fury filled him again.

Go to your room, *she commanded.*

He scurried to the door, turning back just in time to see Ial gripping Ylia's arm. He squinted as a flash of light nearly blinded him and Ylia cried out. Suddenly, his sister's ithlyn glowed far less brightly.

"If you can't handle the responsibility of Light, then you can go without it for a while," Ial hissed. "Don't embarrass me again."

Theren awoke to hands shaking him roughly and he struggled to open his eyes. A slap across the face quickly ameliorated the issue.

His eyes flickered open as he reached for his Light to defend himself but found he was almost entirely drained. A wash of dampened emotion drifted over him; anger, concern, fear, and most strongly, disapproval. That final feeling belonged to Athas, who was standing over him in a stance that suggested he was responsible for the slap. Theren realised where he was; laying on his bed, where he had been when he reached out to Valyn.

"What were you doing? What were you thinking?" Athas scolded.

Theren sat up, feeling weak. He clenched his hands into fists and examined his ithlyn, which glowed only barely against his fair skin.

He looked up to see Talith and Leyen hovering in the doorway.

"I'm sorry. I was practicing," Theren murmured. "Please. Can I go to Ena's spring?"

Theren had never been so depleted of Light before; usually the body prevented overusing its power. Often many men returned from the Brotherwalk fatigued and drawn, their ithlyn barely glowing after months of use and with no chance to restore it. But the only people to exist without Light were those who had committed crimes serious enough to be placed in the cells underground, beneath the roots of Ena's trunk, the Untouchable as they were called. Their minds were entirely disconnected from the spire after the Speaker put them through a ritual that extinguished the Light from their bodies. It was an existence feared by all; surely death would be better than to be cut off from the Light; Light they'd known since birth, from the moment they left the womb and fell into Ena's spring.

Athas was silent a moment, no doubt furiously communing with Talith and Leyen. Theren didn't care. He just wanted to feel his Light again. He tried to stand up and fell back onto the bed. Athas offered him a hand and helped him up. Theren wobbled but kept his feet. He glanced at the sigils on the walls, which appeared unchanged. Hopefully Athas would not know what he had been doing.

"I was training," Theren lied again. "I must have pushed too hard."

Athas gave him a long look, and Theren felt only a whisper of the man's scepticism.

"The whole problem with your training so far," Athas said, "is that you are doing too much." The Dream Master allowed a flicker of frustration to pass over his face, as though Theren was little more than a child. "You need to relax your mind and let go rather than trying to control what comes in and out."

Theren felt his mind shutting itself away, then realised there was no need. His connection with Light was faint enough that it would be hard for Athas to read him.

"Sorry, sir." Theren hung his head.

Athas stepped closer. "I can't help but wonder whether it really was training you were doing, or something else."

"It was nothing, Dream Master. I was just being reckless." Theren tried to send out humility as he continued his lie. "I am frustrated at my slow progress and at being a Dreamer at all," Theren said, feeling a catch in his throat. More words spilled forth as his mind spun. "I hate that I was a Hunter for a moment, and you took it away from me. I want to be able to leave here, to leave the tower, the spire, to venture into the forest -" Theren stopped himself. His lie was fast becoming the truth, and he did not want to share the whole of it; that he wished to stand watch by an ancient sigil at the edge of the Abyss. He took a deep breath. "I want to go on the Brotherwalk."

Athas regarded him in silence for a long moment.

"I think this is a good thing," the Dream Master said after a while. "Without your Light, you are easily tired. It is harder to control your mind. You will need to rest more before resuming training, but I think we will hold off in replenishing your Light for the time being."

"It will help him Tether," Talith remarked, eyes fixed on him. "Good idea, Dream Master."

Athas nodded at Theren — the physical expression another sign of how far he'd slipped in the man's estimation.

"Once you have felt the Tether," Athas said, "I will take you to Ena's spring. You are still physically drained. Rest then and we will return to training tomorrow."

Theren stared at Athas, blinking slowly. The room felt hazy around him. He was lost without his Light.

"No...please Dream Master."

Athas turned to the door, which Leyen practically ran to open for him.

Sorry, Theren.

Theren could barely hear the Dream Master's words in his mind as the man left, Talith close behind him. Leyen stayed at the door, surely still suffering the brunt of Athas' anger for his inattention. Leyen's gaze remained focused on the ground as he hurried after them.

Theren groaned before he slumped back onto his bed and put his head in his hands, exhausted.

Everything was going wrong. He was still trapped in this tower, and now he knew no one would do anything about his Dream. His sigil.

Though it was only afternoon, and he wanted to apologise to Leyen, instead he found himself seduced by the sweet release of sleep. No visions of sigils plagued him, no pull towards the edge of the forest. Just blissful, empty slumber.

Leyen woke him the next morning with a gentle hand on his shoulder, the low light of the room suggesting that the sun had not yet risen.

"Good," Leyen whispered as Theren's eyes flickered open. "You're still alive at least."

Theren sat up, feeling groggy but more alert than the day before. He checked his ithlyn, which of course were still dim.

"I am sorry if I got you in trouble," Theren said. "I just lost control of my Light. I was trying to break down the barriers in my mind that have Athas so annoyed. I hate being slow at this."

A lie was better if you could distract the other party with their own emotions.

"It's alright," Leyen replied. "I made my own choice. I suppose we've both learned a lesson."

Theren sent his agreement and Leyen gave an almost imperceptible nod. Theren closed his eyes and sighed. A nod. Leyen may as well have frowned. Even *he* thought Theren was a child.

"Come on," Leyen encouraged. "Let's get ready. Athas wants us as soon as possible."

Theren looked down at his dimly glowing hands, trepidation filling him. What if Athas was right and his mind was more easily known without the strength from his Light? Everything he had ever hidden would be revealed.

"Leyen," Theren asked as they walked to the bathrooms. "What happens when a Dreamer Tethers...and everyone knows them...and..." He trailed off, uncertain whether it was wise to ask this question.

"What if no-one likes them after?" Leyen finished.

Theren hung his head.

"That hasn't happened," Leyen said. "Though we all feared it before we Tethered." Leyen's gaze turned distant. Theren sensed an echo of the young man's fear, but it was distant. "We were just children. There is no thought or act so bad that a child cannot be forgiven." He glanced at Theren then looked away. Theren thought about what remained unsaid.

Theren was not a child, even though he was not quite a man either, and his secrets were not only his own.

Theren expected them to go straight to the Hall of Echoes, but instead Leyen led him farther up the tower. With no sense of explanation from his companion, Theren was forced to ask aloud what he would have otherwise gleaned from Leyen's mind.

"Where are we going?"

"Athas wants to try something different today."

That was the only explanation offered as they climbed higher, eventually pausing at an opaque engraved door, sigils etched upon the glass. Leyen rested his hand upon the door, but Theren could barely feel the Light working beneath the young man's hands. The door opened, and Theren stepped through to a room of simple but elegant design; crystal chandeliers hung from the high ceiling and woven tapestries depicting scenes in Alvar history decorated the walls. By the arched window sat two large, cushioned chairs that grew out of the crystal floor. Athas sat in one, and the other was empty.

"We'll train in here today," Athas explained.

Leyen left without another word. Theren stood in the middle of the room.

"I am leaving for the Brotherwalk soon," Athas stated, standing as spoke. "The Revel is tomorrow night, and I intend to leave the next morning." His tone communicated all that Theren's disconnected mind could not feel. Consternation. Theren didn't speak.

"I would feel better about leaving if I know you have Tethered. The rest can wait. You do not need to master your Dreamer abilities, but your mind needs the safety of the Tether. Of your fellow Dreamers."

Fellow Dreamers. They may all have shared the same title, but Theren felt no affinity for them. Speaking with Ylia, and feeling Valyn's fleeting presence, reminded him of all he wanted; to be a Hunter, and to be among family.

That, and to answer the call to the edge of the forest. Even without his Light, it remained just as strong.

"I will try," Theren said. "I am trying, sir."

Athas gestured to the seat in front of him. Theren joined him by the window, looking out over the glowing city below.

"How do you feel?" Athas asked, glancing at Theren's faded ithlyn.

"Empty," Theren replied.

Athas was quiet a moment before he spoke again. "Do you know what happens to those who defy Ena's laws?"

Theren's chest squeezed tight as his mind cycled through memories of his and Valyn's every transgression.

"Of course," he replied nonchalantly. "The Speaker removes their Light, cuts them off from the spire, and holds them under the city."

Athas remained impassive. "That is not the entire truth. Without Light, we die. Once we are touched by an Entity, we are forever reliant on their power. It is why, instinctively, your body will never let you use it up completely." He fixed Theren with a serious expression, and a faint sense of worry and regret touched at the edges of Theren's mind. "The ritual to remove a person's ability to use Light is risky. Many don't survive."

Questions sprung up in Theren's mind, not in the least why this wasn't common knowledge. Perhaps, because transgressions were so rare, it was easy to hide this fact.

"But those that do," Athas continued, "are left so weak, their Light so faint — just a shred of Ena's power within them — that they are easy to contain. They may feel whispers of those above; their loved ones, the height of a Revel when the frenzy of emotion is high... But no one hears them. And there is not enough Light left within them to use."

"Why are you telling me this?" Theren asked.

"Try to use your Light, Theren."

Theren's stomach sank. With effort, he held his hand aloft and a faint ball of light glowed from his palm. Though he was relieved he could still conjure it, the action should not have been so hard.

"You are but a hairsbreadth away from being in the same state as those who are held beneath the spire." Athas sighed. "And you did that to yourself. I fail to see what manner of training you were doing that brought you so close to the brink of death." Theren didn't say a word, counting his breaths until Athas spoke again. "What did you do?"

Theren's mind scrambled as he composed another lie; a lie that would be easier to tell now that Athas would not be able to feel him.

"I was trying to find the Tether," Theren said finally. "But I didn't know what I was doing. I just flared my Light and tried to repeat the exercises we were doing in the Hall of Echoes. It was chaos. I was just so frustrated!"

Athas regarded him for a long time, the silence of the room gnawing as Theren hoped Athas wouldn't see the truth. If anyone asked Valyn, he hoped she would repeat his message. And Ylia? What if she revealed what he had done? She might, if she was worried he was going mad.

"I want you to know this is not a thing I do lightly," Athas explained. "I can't imagine the emptiness you are experiencing, disconnected from Ena as you are. But though I wish to let you bathe in Ena's spring and restore yourself, I can't until you Tether."

"Why?"

Athas continued as though Theren hadn't spoken. "Talith and the others will keep working with you, but many of our number will soon be gone on the Brotherwalk. I can't risk you having full access to your power until we can properly monitor you."

Theren's gut twisted. Athas feared the Dreamer's madness. That's what the Tether truly was. They could paint it as a humbling connection, a comfortable belonging that tied the Dreamers to one another so they could share the burden of their Dreams. But it was nothing more than surveillance; an enhanced version of the spire's interconnection that Theren had managed to avoid for so long. He did not mind opening himself to Valyn, or his sister, or Roshin. But in this, he would not be able to choose who he was close to. Anyone would have access to his mind and memories. He'd be nothing more than a Dreamer, and a poor one at that, whose wants came second to that of the whole.

The image of the sigil at the edge of the forest floated behind his eyes once more, and in his mind's eye, stars spun above him like he was standing out in the open field of the Abyss. This was not a sacrifice he was willing to make. He had lived separately for too long. He did not belong. Perhaps he was already mad? What was the first step down the path to madness if not the rejection of normality?

Athas spoke. "Of course, I would prefer to see you restored in Ena's spring before I leave. Are you open to trying something new?"

Theren searched Athas' impassive face. Though a faint sense of urgency and reassurance brushed over his mind, Theren knew whatever Athas wanted to try would fail. In his heart, he did not want to Tether.

"I think I need some time," Theren stammered, sending out uncertainty and hoping that Athas would feel it. "I don't think I am ready to be a Dreamer, Dream Master."

"And yet you nearly killed yourself trying to Tether?" Athas said. A hint of suspicion drifted between them. A familiar cold fear flooded Theren as he realised he had erred. His mind turned in on itself. He would have to submit.

"What do I have to do?" Theren murmured.

"Nothing," Athas replied. "I will do it. Let me in, just like when you shared the Dream. I can link you to the Tether."

Then everyone would know him, know all his faults, all of Valyn's secrets, and Ylia's transgressions in helping him. What would the Dreamers think of their future Speaker when they learned that she didn't follow the rules? What would they think of him when they knew how weak his mind was?

"Alright," Theren replied almost inaudibly as his mind drifted away.

Somewhere, he felt Athas rest a hand on his shoulder. Athas was going to force him to Tether.

Theren lost himself for a moment, feeling all at once within and beside himself, searching, grasping. All he knew were clouds drifting over an open sky and freedom from the spire.

Faintly, he realised that Athas was calling his name. Aloud.

He blinked and looked around the room. Athas' concern was written on his face.

"I don't understand." Athas shook his head before slumping back into the chair. "Your mind...it's like you aren't there. I've never seen anything like this."

Strange. Broken. Theren huffed a laugh. Growing up, Valyn always thought she was the defective one. If only she knew.

"I'm sorry," Theren murmured. "Maybe it's too late?" Maybe he was too old to become a Dreamer. Another thought niggled at him; maybe was already infected with the Dreamers madness.

Athas stood and gazed out the window. "I don't accept that. Ena would not do this to you. We just need more time to understand, and it is time I do not have."

Theren did not suggest that perhaps Athas could simply miss the Brotherwalk. It was not an option. The Dream Master must attend. And, if Theren were honest, he didn't want Athas close to him anymore.

He didn't want anyone close to him anymore.

"I think I need to rest," Theren said. "Don't feel bad about the Light. It's alright. It's for the best."

Theren tried not to run from the room, ignoring Athas' half-hearted call. Thankfully, the Dream Master did not follow.

18

Theren and Valyn sat on a branch above Starspire looking down on the glistening city below as the last of Ena's daylight glow faded.

"Do you put your amulet back on sometimes?" Valyn asked, her legs swinging enthusiastically beneath them as she dangled them over the branch.

It took a moment for Theren to realise she was talking about the amulet they wore as children; which he'd not worn for a few years short of a decade now.

"No, of course not. I don't know if it even works anymore," he replied. Valyn nodded. "Why?" he asked, sensing her attempt to quiet her mind. He could intrude but that would be unfair. Besides, he knew how much he hated it when it was done to him.

"Sometimes I can't find you," Valyn answered finally.

That was the thing about avoiding being overheard. If you got good enough at being quiet, you could think and feel so little that it was like you didn't even exist.

No one could use your thoughts against you that way.

The day passed in a weary haze as Theren laid in solitude in his room. He dozed, his body still recovering from the ordeal of using up so much of his Light. He avoided falling asleep properly; though it was a tempting escape from reality, he feared new Dreams arising. Alas, it was clear the first Dream was not done with him; the edge of the forest was still in his mind's eye and the persistent tug in his gut gnawed at him. He could almost ignore it, but it was never truly gone. Strangely, he didn't want it gone. It almost felt a part of him now.

Was that his first Dream? He wondered about his dream as a boy, the one that had sent his mother into a paranoid rage. What would have happened if she had died on that journey? Would Ylia have stepped up into the Speaker's role early? He supposed so. With fervour, he believed she would have been a good Speaker even as a child. She had been a good sister. She was still a good sister, risking much to let him listen in to the Council. He didn't know why she was so kind to him.

No one bothered him until Leyen announced himself at the door, his presence vague but still detectable despite Theren's weak power. With so much rest, Theren felt his body adjusting to the lack of Light. It was still a hollow, lifeless feeling, to be so depleted, but at least now he could stand without the room spinning.

When Theren opened the door, it was not only Leyen waiting for him on the other side. Beside him stood one of the young Dreamer apprentices, a boy perhaps only a year off from his own Brotherwalk. Leyen and Theren exchanged greetings before Leyen introduced the boy.

"This is Eles," he said, and the boy offered a formal greeting. "He will be taking my place."

"Why?" Theren asked, surprised.

Though he could not feel Leyen's discomfort, the silence conveyed it. "I will be busy tonight. And leaving tomorrow."

The Revel. And the Brotherwalk. Theren straightened his back. They were leaving a child to watch over his sleep while all the other men were gone.

"Very well," he replied before returning Eles' greeting. "If you'll excuse me," he continued. "I am going to break my fast."

He pushed past them and made his way up the stairs. He was breathing hard by the time he reached the top, but he refused to let his Light-lacking body slow him. Perhaps it was a good thing to live with limited Light for a while. He was weak without it. Not to mention, being disconnected from those in the Tower and Starspire at large meant he would be almost impossible to sense. His mind was his own again.

Theren filled a plate with food, paying no attention to his selection, and went to stand by the open arches. He picked listlessly at his meal, instead taking in the city beneath him; beautiful to the eye yet absent in his mind.

Strangely, for usually no wind penetrated this deep through the forest, a breeze wafted in through the window, ruffling his hair. It smelt of dried grass and sunshine, and Theren recalled days sitting in the branches beside the open fields of the forest's edge. It was sun-season in the land beyond the forest, perfect for watching the starry sky in the night air — even warmer than the ever-mild climate of the spire.

Theren put the plate on the sill and closed his eyes. Longing pulled at him, as though he was a fish on the end of a hook, being tugged towards an end that was futile to fight.

He did not want to fight it. He wanted it.

A smile lifted the corner of his lips. Perhaps he was looking at his situation incorrectly. After all, there were benefits to being disconnected from everyone in the spire.

Theren had the vaguest sense of Talith's and Athas' confusion for the rest of that day, as they saw a newfound ease within him. He spoke freely with the other Dreamers, joked with Eles, and spoke of the Revel and the impending departure for the Brotherwalk. In the bright glow of mid-afternoon, he was found at a table taking tisane with a group of young male Dreamers.

"We have all been reluctant to speak of the Brotherwalk in front of you," Leyen remarked, to the agreement of the others. "It feels unfair that you are unable to go, though of course, I understand Athas' reasoning."

"It is unfair," another man agreed.

"I must admit, I fought the decision at first." Theren sighed. "But now I see, it is simply the way things must be," Theren reassured them, projecting a false calm that he knew they would barely sense. "I will just live through your stories instead. You must be excited?" He leaned back in his chair and took a sip of his tisane, trying to keep his eyes from flickering to the open arches at the edge of the room. The forest called to him.

Soon, he thought, grateful there was no chance anyone could overhear his thoughts. He refocused on the conversation around him.

The eldest of the group had undertaken five Brotherwalks, and Leyen was embarking on only his second. They shared tales of the beauty of the other spires and the Light of the other Alvar cities, representing all the colours of the rainbow.

The spires' beauty was not the only thing discussed. Theren was pleased his discomfort was so easily hidden as they described their nights in soft beds with lovers who some yearned to see again and others they hoped to avoid. Leyen could not hide the blush that stained his pale face when he described how he'd blundered through his first courtship. Theren felt his cheeks heat as he imagined his own likely failure at such things.

"Ah, Leyen," someone joked, clasping the man's shoulder. "I'm sure it was not so bad."

Theren sent out mirth, knowing it would hardly be felt. Without his Light to express himself, he tried to exude nonchalance; a man relaxed, cheerful, at peace.

"At least I don't have to worry about that for one more year," he said.

The men's humour was palpable, intermingled with their own relief at his acceptance. They believed him. Theren had made his peace with his fate, and they could relax around him — finally.

"Next year, when your Dreamer powers are fully under your command, we'll leave with you on the morning of your first Brotherwalk," one of the men offered.

"Better late than never, yes?" another added.

Theren flashed a brief smile, a childish act for which he could sense instant forgiveness. For, of course, he was still a child to them; a boy, barely in control of his Dreamer powers. One they were leaving behind, adequately guarded by another child.

It was strange having someone in the room other than Leyen that night. Theren realised he had become accustomed to the young man's presence. Could he call Leyen a friend? Perhaps, though Theren hadn't treated him much like one. He pushed aside the guilt at how he'd convinced Leyen to leave him the day he'd spied on the Council. It had been worth it. It had been necessary.

Theren lay awake, relying as much on his physical senses as his mental ones to discern when Eles had fallen asleep. It took a long time. Theren did not blame the lad; even with the barriers of the Dreamers' sigils, the feel of the Revel thrummed through the glass. Theren barely felt it, but he knew what it sounded like. It was a familiar sense, one all the children old enough to remove their amulets tolerated for a few months a year until they, too, could join the festivities. The first Revel of the Brotherwalk season was the only night that men and women of the same spire were permitted flirtation with each other; drunk on Light Wine, the dancing and repartee all in practice for the upcoming festivities of the Brotherwalk. Some men even left in the night, full of Ena's Light and high on celebration. Not long after dawn, all the men who could leave would be gone.

And, when the time came tomorrow, Theren intended to be one of them. It was a thought he didn't have to shield too carefully since few would be paying attention to him. Athas, Talith, Leyen, and all the other adult Dreamers would be at the Revel. Eles was among the oldest Dreamers left in the tower. And he was asleep.

Theren quietly pushed back his covers and stole from the room. The tower was silent, the sigils glittering along the walls of the opaque, pale blue glass. Barefoot, Theren hurried to the communal room at the top of the tower, panting heavily by the time he reached the arches. He took a moment to catch his breath. Though Feldan often forced them to rely on physical prowess alone while Hunting, and Theren's full draw of a bow was impressive without the aid of his Light, it was another thing entirely to exist without power. Errantly, Theren wondered what the Listeners knew of this; in what other ways did Light enhance their lives without their awareness?

Theren shook the thought from his mind and stepped up to the threshold of the window. Now was not the time. The city was dizzying beneath him. The Revel felt like a distant tapestry of minds, full of merriment and joy. He should have been down there, along with his friends. Valyn would be there, though perhaps reluctantly. Instinctively he almost reached out to her, but realised it would be pointless. He was too depleted to be able to reach her properly, and besides, he didn't want to draw attention to himself. He was keenly aware that he could not rely on his Light to assist him in his journey out of the Tower this night. With one misplaced hand, one slip of the foot, he would plummet to his death.

He hesitated; perhaps this was folly.

The thought was quickly overtaken by the memory of the sigil at the forest's edge. An urgent pull overcame him, as familiar now as his own breathing. He stepped off the ledge without another thought. Newly energised, he hurried across the rooftops of Starspire, his indigo Dreamer's robe a dark shadow against the glowing backdrop of the city at night.

He took a circuitous route to the Speaker's Tower, stowing along empty streets, over bridges, across rooftops, and climbing walls. His muscles protested and he stopped often to catch his breath, but determination drove him until he finally alighted through the window of his old room in Ylia's apartment. Out of habit, he drew his mind into himself, keeping quiet as he took in the room. It was as he left it, as though he would return any day to sleep soundly beneath his ceiling of stars. Gazing up, he smiled. He would see those stars for real tonight.

Quickly, he changed into a shirt and breeches and fitted his leather armour over the top. The forest might be his haunt, but he was not a fool. It was wild; and even the most familiar wilds could bring you to harm. When he slipped out through the window once more, he left with his crystal bow and leather quiver over his shoulder and a long-knife on his belt.

No one was the wiser as he stowed out of the city.

The forest appeared as it always did at night. The darkness was punctuated by the veins of Ena's light in the earth, the trees, and the gentle glow of the foliage. As Theren ran across the branches, he was struck with a deep sense of protectiveness. His shoulders tensed and his heart skipped a beat as a wave of furious heat crashed through him; he would do anything to keep this forest safe.

Theren didn't stop to ponder the feeling. Safe from what? Rarely did a Light-mad beast ever threaten Starspire, but they belonged to the forest; an unfortunate malady but no more serious than a dead branch that needed to be pruned from a shrub.

No, it was the forest, not the spire, he felt fierce about. And nothing had ever threatened that save the Void. The Void were gone though, vanquished so long ago that even the Listeners had forgotten almost everything about them. No one even recalled what they looked like. Not that Theren knew of, anyway. If he'd learned anything since The Choosing, it was that there was much to life in the spire of which he was ignorant.

Once he had put enough distance between himself and the spire, he paused against a tree to catch his breath. His eyelids were heavy but he refused to succumb to sleep. He rested his head against the rough bark and removed a glove to examine his ithlyn. In the night's gloom the lines of Light on his skin were more visible than in the brightness of Starspire. He conjured a small flame in the air, dismissing it quickly. It was little reassurance to know he could still do that minor trick; it would not serve him if he were to face down a forest beast. He thought of his secret trips out of the city as a boy — sometimes with Valyn, sometimes alone. He did not fear.

This was where he needed to be; in the forest among the trees and wild animals. Not cooped up in the Dreamers' Tower like a criminal. Not Tethered to the minds of others, surrendering his autonomy and subsumed into a greater whole. Out of the spire, in the forest, he felt complete.

Once he had recovered, he set back off into the night with only a glance behind in the direction he'd come. He wondered fleetingly what would happen if he never returned.

Finally, he arrived at the edge of the forest where the inky sky stretched endlessly above and the soft glow of the trees gave way to the velvet shadows of the Abyss. With the knowledge of instinct, he knew he was at the same spot where his Dream had taken place. The pull in his chest subsided and he sighed in relief, as though he had been holding his breath for a lifetime and only just learned to exhale.

Theren climbed higher through the trees to check the sigil, which remained unchanged, before he found a suitable crook of a branch in which to settle. He stowed his weapons and sat down, one leg dangling as he looked out over the Abyss as though he was taking up watch. His breathing slowed as his eyes roamed over the monochrome fields. What was out there, he wondered? How long had it been since an Alvar had set foot in the open air?

Questions danced across his mind as he dozed softly, a sense of peace settling over him.

19

The twinkle of starlight was a unique beauty, Theren thought, as he gazed out over the Abyss into the night sky.

It's beautiful, *Valyn whispered in his mind. Her presence was soft beside him, for once. No anger, no resentment, no angst. He shuffled closer to her and she rested her head on his shoulder.*

Imagine running through those fields, *Valyn remarked, sharing a vision of the two of them racing down the hill before them, tumbling as they tripped in the grass.*

Caution tweaked his stomach; wariness of the open sky had been strongly impressed on him. The men who had taken him to the edge of the forest were free in sharing their fear. Yet, despite Theren sharing those experiences with Valyn, she didn't seem to care.

She was all awe and inspiration. Theren shoved the fear aside.

I wonder how far we could run?

Theren awoke to sunlight on his face and blinked as it flickered through the leaves of the trees. He knew where he was immediately, the sense of peace he'd found last night still resting in his chest. Part of him was saddened that he had not spent longer stargazing, but there was little need to worry. He would have countless nights to lose himself in the night sky. He was not intending to return to the spire.

He stood and stretched, his muscles stiff from a night of poor posture. He kept his mind quiet, hoping no one would sense where he was. He was certain that by the time people realised he had vanished, most of the men able to search for him would have already left on the Brotherwalk. None would be coming this way; the only other spire in this direction was Shadowspire, to the East, but to travel as the bird flies would require crossing the Abyss. None would risk that. Theren was safe from accidental discovery, and a search party was unlikely to look for him. They would surely assume he had left for the Brotherwalk anyway.

Theren hadn't even considered it. He needed to be here.

Recalling the sense of intrusion from his Dream, he jumped down several branches and alighted on the ground to examine the dirt as though he were tracking a beast. There were few tracks that crossed the tree line; creatures of Ena rarely left the purview of their Entity to explore the lesser forests, let alone the open fields. There was nothing amiss, the same as that night when he had investigated his Dream.

He climbed up to the sigil and examined its glowing pattern, resting his palm against it. Questions flurried around his mind as he imagined who may have placed it there and how long ago. That the Listeners didn't rush to research the sigil was a greater affront than his exclusion from the Brotherwalk. A piece of their lost history was awaiting discovery, and no one appeared to care.

There was time, they had said in the Council meeting. They would research it when the men returned. Though it made sense on some level, it was an unsatisfying excuse. It felt more urgent than that.

Theren let his hand slide slowly off the sigil and wondered. Even though it felt urgent, it wasn't. There was nothing out here.

Which meant the Dream was surely a memory of the past, like Athas had discerned and the Council agreed. And Theren had breached the rules of the spire and left without permission. For nothing.

Athas' words of warning crossed his mind. 'Investigating a Dream, obsessing over it, is a step down a path from which you cannot return.'

No. Theren's eyes were open. He knew how he felt.

Doubt gnawed quietly at him as he set about gathering himself some breakfast.

Surviving in the forest was no easy feat, but Theren would have been doing it anyway if he had gone on the Brotherwalk. He and the other boys had trained their whole lives to survive the journey from spire to spire, and the best of those were chosen as Hunters to protect their home. The forest connected to Ena provided food in abundance. It was once you left the shelter of her trees and entered the lesser forests that food grew scarcer.

Theren set up a hidden campsite tucked in the roots of the large trees. He was faced with a problem. Where on the Brotherwalk he would have used his Light to make fire or provide shelter, he now found himself without that luxury.

Without our Light, we are useless, he thought to himself as he stared at the circle of rocks he'd laid out for a fire. He was not entirely without power, though, and he was becoming more comfortable with the empty feeling as the days progressed and his body took on the challenge of limited Light. *Perhaps this is a good thing*, he wondered. If he could learn to live without Light, it would surely make him stronger. Better prepared.

For what?

"I don't know," he replied aloud to himself. He set about sharpening a stick to skewer the forest vegetables he'd foraged. He had enough Light to sustain a small fire but he was loath to start it yet. Even small acts using his Light were immensely draining now, and after Athas' words of caution, he could admit to some fear about being so close to losing his Light altogether. Did people really die without it? Yet another of the

Speaker's secrets and the cruelty of her immense power over them all.

At least Ylia was good. Perhaps she could change Starspire for the better. If she could listen to Valyn's ideas and loosen some of the traditions the Alvar clung to, maybe they could make a better world. It was not as though this one was so bad, but a world in which Valyn could be happier was worth the change.

Theren rested his skewered vegetables between the tree roots and made his way to the forest's edge. All morning he kept finding himself standing there, looking out onto the broken spire below. It was a clear, bright day, and the heat from the sun reflected off the waving grass. He crouched and ran his gloved fingers over the green strands before removing his gloves to repeat the action. The grass was silky against his skin, and, with nowhere else to be, he luxuriated in the moment. The fields moved like rippling water in the gentle breeze.

He considered taking a few steps outside the tree line. His fear was irrational, he knew. A legacy of generations had left him frightened of an open sky, the feeling shared from each mind to the next.

A shift in the air of the forest behind him brushed against his consciousness. Theren spun, stepping behind a tree trunk, heart racing. He looked to his campsite where his long-knife sat. His bow and quiver were hidden in the tree above.

"Theren?" a familiar voice said aloud. Theren hesitated only a moment before stepping out from the trees. Valyn's face lit up at the sight of him, as though they were children once again and he had arrived at her house to play. She rushed forward and embraced him, her arms tight around his body. When they stepped apart, concern flickered across her face.

"Your ithlyn!" She took his hands and traced her thumb across the dim lines of light. "What did they do to you?"

"I, err, sort of did this to myself," Theren replied.

Valyn glared at him and tossed his hands aside. "What is going on?" He could barely feel her anger, but her face made it clear how she felt. "I can hardly feel you at all. It's almost like you're wearing an amulet."

"Did anyone come with you?" Theren asked, looking past her into the soft gloom of the forest.

Valyn shook her head. "No," she replied. "Everyone assumes you went on the Brotherwalk. The men are all on the lookout for you on their travels."

He regarded her solemnly, relieved at the men's assumption. Where else would a boy of age yearn to go?

"But you knew where I was," he murmured.

Valyn held his gaze. "I did. When you reached out to me the day of the Council meeting, I could feel everything you felt, for a moment anyway. It was...intense." She frowned at him. "And I had the Dream, too, remember? Thanks to you..." Her eyes grew distant for a moment. "I don't remember the details, only the feeling yanking me towards the Abyss. I can't forget that."

"I'm sorry." Theren rubbed his neck, not sure what to make of her recollection. If Valyn had known where he was, surely anyone else who had felt the dream might also suspect. "You must be relieved that it's me cursed to be a Dreamer and not you."

Valyn rolled her eyes. "Everyone is blaming me for it, anyway, saying that somehow I must have brought this on you."

"Really?"

"It doesn't matter," she dismissed his question. "What are you doing out here with no Light? Are you crazy?"

Her tone suggested the latter question was not rhetorical.

"I'm not," he replied. "I..." He trailed off.

"Because this seems crazy to me." She frowned. "You've run off from the spire, told no one where you were going, and all for what? A feeling?"

"It's...it's not just a feeling," Theren stammered. "I just have to be here."

"Why?"

"I just do."

"That's not a reason."

Theren took her hand suddenly and tried to connect to her. Their link was difficult, distant, but he exhaled and made the choice to release his mind; to be known. Maybe he was crazy, fallen to the Dreamers madness. Maybe he was no longer able to discern what was real and what was invented in his mind. Valyn would know. He wanted her to know.

He felt the litany of Valyn's emotions that followed; shock, fear, grief, and, finally, a warm acceptance of everything he was.

"Come here, you idiot," Valyn murmured, pulling him into a hug again.

"You don't think I've got the Dreamers' madness?"

"I don't know." Valyn's voice was muffled against his shoulder. "I can barely feel you, but from what I can? You feel like Theren to me."

Something inside him shifted at those words, and he felt a broken part of him come together. Valyn knew him. He *could* connect with others, be one with them, as long as there was a choice.

"I just need a while away from the spire to figure out why Ena wants me here," Theren explained as they parted and he led her to his campsite. Valyn was silent as she started a fire and created several orbs of light to float above them. Theren placed his vegetables across the flames and began roasting his lunch.

"I won't tell anyone where you are. No one knows I'm here. But, Theren..." She fixed a serious gaze upon him. "Someone will wonder. Ylia knows about your Dream. The other Dreamers, too, yes?"

Theren sent his confirmation then nodded, realising it was easier to communicate with gesture now.

"They could send a group of boys out to look for you here. I don't think it's safe."

Theren hadn't considered that. "Do you know what the Speaker thinks?"

Valyn appeared to consider her words carefully. "It was not your mother who was leading the search for you today."

Of course not, he thought to himself. Ial wanted him on the Brotherwalk so he didn't shame her.

"Mother asked me where I thought you were and I lied. It is so hard to lie to her, Theren." Her breathing quickened. "I'm not like you. I can be read much more easily. I think I'm going to ruin this for you."

"It's alright," he reassured her, though he felt a measure of worry. It didn't matter whether Valyn was easier to read. If Ial wanted to know something, or Ylia, they need only force themselves in.

"What will happen if they find you out here?" she asked. "What will the Dreamers do?"

Theren thought of what Athas had said and tried to do. They would pin him to the Tether, force themselves into his mind. And if he was truly mad, well, perhaps he faced a lifetime of sitting in a cell beneath the spire with most of the Light sucked from his body. Or maybe he would be killed from whatever ritual his mother put him through. He wasn't sure which between the two options seemed the kinder.

"It's not good," he replied.

Valyn straightened her shoulders as though that settled something for her.

"In that case, I've got an idea."

"Oh?"

"You're going to love it."

The mischievous grin on her face suggested that might not be true.

"Tell me."

Valyn took a deep breath and held Theren's gaze.

"I'll go on the Brotherwalk for you."

20

Theren and Valyn sat by the warmheart; their minds silenced by the amulets on their wrists. Roshin watched over them from the kitchen, an absent smile on her face.

Valyn stood up in a rush, tripped, and accidentally hit her head on the warmheart. The quiet 'thud' preceded a barrage of tears. Roshin put her towel down and took a step forward before she looked up and saw Valyn gathered in Theren's arms.

"There, there," he murmured, rubbing Valyn's head. "It'll stop hurting soon."

Roshin's eyes watered, and she hung back, watching. Valyn's sobs slowly subsided.

"Do you need a hug from mama?" Roshin called, unable to help herself.

"Yes," Valyn called.

Roshin came over and gathered both children in her arms.

"Theren's very wise," she murmured into Valyn's hair. "Pain doesn't last forever. And while it's there..." She moved to place a kiss on Theren's brow. *"We have to take care of each other."*

Theren sat, stunned, as he listened to Valyn's plan.

"I will sneak out of the spire."

"But, Val —"

"Hush, let me finish. I will go on the Brotherwalk, just like you would have. I will dress like a man — my hair is short anyway — and pretend I am you when I reach the other spires. I will act normally — don't you say it — and everyone will see that Theren Ialson, son of the Speaker of Starspire, is perfectly sane."

The fire cooking Theren's lunch danced beside them, the light flickering across Valyn's face in a manner that made Theren wonder if *she* was not the mad one. He could not tear his eyes away from his friend as he listened to her plan.

"If your mother reaches out to commune with any of the other Speakers," Valyn continued, "she will hear word of your journey. No one will suspect you are sitting here, barely an hour away from Starspire, and I won't be around for your mother or Ylia to interrogate."

"Valyn, that plan is madder than I might be," Theren shook his head, turning the vegetables over the flames. "Where will everyone think you have gone? What will you do if there are visitors from Starspire at the same spire you're at? They'll know you're not me."

"I will connect with Mother before I leave Ena's forest and tell her I've gone to look for you. She won't be able to tell it is a lie if I keep it brief."

"You'll break her heart," Theren murmured. Her two children, both gone.

"She'll understand in the end." Valyn waved his words away. "And as to the second point, I will do my best to figure out who is visiting when I arrive. The spires are big places. If I only stay briefly at each, the risk of being discovered is minimal. I was thinking I might go to Skyspire first..."

Theren narrowed his eyes as Valyn rambled about her proposed journey. She had given it a great deal of thought.

"You aren't doing this just for me," Theren realised. "You want to go on the Brotherwalk."

Valyn drew herself up. "And why shouldn't I? It sounds fun."

"You're not trained to survive in the wilds!"

"You trained me," she replied simply, as though that would end the argument.

"I told you *some* of it!" Theren threw his hands up, any pretence of hiding his expressions forgotten. "Valyn, it's not a game. You must find food, and the creatures beyond Ena's reach are wild and unpredictable."

"You told me all that already." Valyn shrugged. "I know I've never gone on a Hunt, and I know there's risk. But I can do this, Theren. I want to prove I can. And this way, we can both have what we want."

Theren stared at her for long moments. There were so many flaws to this plan. Valyn could so easily be harmed, or lost, or discovered by any of the men from Starspire and hauled back home to face his mother for an egregious breach of tradition.

"Let me do this for you, Theren," Valyn said, sending forth the full force of her determination. "Why should Dreamers live separately? Why should I have to stay and face ridicule from everyone for being a little different?" She held his gaze. "It was you who told me I was too angry and that I never did anything with it."

"I'm sorry for what I said," Theren interjected.

"No, you were right. And you're right to run away from the Dreamers. I can't believe Athas is letting you walk around with almost no Light! That's cruel!"

"Better a Dreamer go mad without his Light to harm others," Theren mused dryly.

Valyn opened her mouth to make a comment but held simply exhaled slowly instead.

"I won't go if you need me to stay here to check on you," she offered. "But I am worried someone will figure it out — that either Mother or Ylia will discover you. Leaving seems the best option."

"I can't ask you to do this for me," Theren said.

"Then don't, and just let me do it for both of us."

Theren gazed at the fire. "Do you think I'm mad? Do I feel different?" He needed to be sure.

Valyn tossed a twig into the fire and frowned. "You're hard to sense. And I don't know what Dreamers' madness feels like. Have you noticed anything unusual?"

"This whole week has been unusual," Theren muttered. "I was a Hunter for less than a day, I've been locked up, gossiped about, I failed miserably at being a Dreamer..." His voice croaked as pressure built in his chest, but he pressed on. "I have sat with this unsettled longing, wanting nothing more than to run from the spire and watch the Abyss. I have missed you, and your mother, and Elska, Ylia...and all the while wondered whether I'm going insane."

Valyn rested her hand on his forearm, and Theren's racing heart slowed.

"Theren." She spoke his name softly, almost as tenderly as Roshin might have. "The Dream means a lot to you; I can feel that. I don't think it's madness to follow a Dream. Maybe you're meant to discover something no one else knows?"

Theren looked away, eyes roaming over the roots of the tree beside them. A little group of mushrooms glowed among the moss tucked against the tree. The leaves overhead cast their pale light upon them. The forest twinkled with Ena's Light, imbued in the very ground beneath them. Surely Ena would not do this to him for no reason?

Theren looked back to Valyn, feeling suddenly resolute.

"Be safe out there," he said. "And don't seduce too many women." Valyn's blush was visible alongside the distant recoil of embarrassment within her.

"I wouldn't. Anyway, no woman will want me once they find out I'm not the prestigious Speaker's son. Emphasis on the 'son'." Valyn stared at the fire, her chin on her knee as she plucked the leaves off a twig.

Theren thought back to something Roshin had said. "I think maybe you'll find more people share your desires than you think." Valyn glanced at him, but she didn't hold his gaze. "You're not strange, Val. I think perhaps secrets are easier to keep in the spire than we realise."

Valyn smiled slightly and got to her feet. "Well, I'm not taking any chances with *my* secrets." Theren stood up, holding his breath as he faced their final goodbye. No, he resolved, it would not be final. He would see her again.

"Wait here," she said, as though he had anywhere else to go. "I'll be back in a while."

She turned and leapt up to a nearby branch, bounding with ease higher into the canopy until she disappeared into the gloom. She was graceful, effortless, at one with the forest.

Perhaps she could survive in the wilds.

Theren was dozing by the low flames of his fire by the time Valyn returned. Night was falling, the glow of the forest stark in the twilight air. Theren jumped to his feet, startled by the sudden sound of her appearance. He'd let his guard down. She was dressed in breeches and good boots, along with a shirt and thick cloak that allowed free movement. Men's clothes, like she always wore, but not quite fit for a hunt. She owned no leathers, for there was no need for a woman to wear armour. Slung over her shoulder was a large satchel, which she dropped to the ground. It clanked.

Theren raised an eyebrow at her.

"I got you some things," she said with a grin. She crouched down and opened the satchel. Inside was an array of useful items, among them: a warmheart, an urn, a thick blanket, and a dagger. "These will hopefully make your stay out here more comfortable."

"Val…"

"And finally…" Her grin widened as she fished something from her shirt pocket. She held her hand closed over it and stepped up close to him. "I think this might come in handy too."

She opened his palm and placed something cool inside it. When he looked down, he saw he now held a leather bracelet in his hand with a sigil-carved gemstone set within. It glowed softly in the darkness. A child's amulet.

"Is this yours?" he asked.

"Yes, Mother kept it."

"Does it still work?" Theren examined the stone against the light of the dimming fire, and Valyn waved her hand to create some light. "Don't!" Theren pushed her hand away. "Conserve your Light for your journey. You'll need every bit you have."

"It works," Valyn confirmed as she pulled her hand into her cloak. "I checked the sigil and imbued it with more Light. If you wore that, even fully restored, no one would be able to sense you."

Theren stared at the amulet. With it, he could sneak into the city, renew his Light, and leave again. As long as he remained out of sight, no one would be the wiser. It was genius.

He looked back at his friend, her smug smile a familiar expression, but her straight back and proud posture something new. Though she felt distant, he could feel something different about her. Something determined, lighter. He lamented his lack of Light for preventing him from truly understanding what was going on with her.

"Why are you doing all this?" he asked. "You seem...different?"

Valyn shrugged and began tying the satchel back up.

"Everything's different. Before, I saw the future laid out — inevitable. You would be a Hunter, probably Hunt Master one day, gone for several months of the year with lovers hanging off your arms once you got over your first time." Theren squirmed. "Your sister would be the Speaker, with a place set for you on the Council. And me? The same as always. Living with questions about the way things could be different but with no way to change them. No way to change me."

Theren opened his mouth to protest that he would never have discarded her like that, but Valyn stopped him.

"It was melancholy thinking, Theren. Not a premonition. Or a Dream." She winked at him. "But now? Everything we assumed would happen has been blown away with one strange twist of fate. There are other possibilities if I am willing to be brave. I will be my own fate. Just like you are now." She chuckled. "Besides, now that you're a pariah like me, I can't have you being the strangest one out of the two of us."

Theren found himself lost for words. It was as though someone had replaced his friend with another soul entirely.

Suspicious, he narrowed his eyes. "Are you real?"

Valyn laughed. "Of course, I'm real."

Theren grabbed her arms and squeezed her gently. "You're not just something I'm Dreaming? Am I asleep?"

"Cut that out." Valyn's humour faded. "I'm real, you're awake, and you're not crazy."

Isn't that what a Dream version of Valyn would say? Theren thought to himself. He began recalling his day, trying to remember what he had been doing before Valyn returned. Had he been asleep?

Valyn shoved him. "Stop. If you're not mad now, you'll make yourself mad by thinking about it too much."

Theren dismissed his worries. He had a more immediate one to deal with.

"Fine. Thank you for this...for everything," he said. "But there are some things you need to take."

He took off his gloves and began untying his leather vest.

"You need that," Valyn objected.

"You need it more," he replied. "These too." He handed her his gloves and finished removing his armour.

"These don't fit," Valyn said, batting at the additional length of fabric beyond the end of her fingers inside the gloves. "You keep them."

Theren frowned but took the gloves back, passing her the vest instead and making her put it on without his help. It was slightly too big but it was serviceable. It wouldn't save her life if an ogyr wanted to bite her head off, but it might help her survive a rock-cat's swipe long enough to stick a knife in it.

They stepped back and regarded each other for a long moment.

"Just goodbye for now, yes?" Theren said, finally.

"Just like we would have said anyway, if things had worked out how had you hoped."

They embraced, Theren's heart twisting as he felt her push at their connection, enhancing her feelings and, he hoped, allowing her to better feel his. He wanted her to know how much he had missed her.

"In a few moons, they'll be touting your name as the greatest lover in Alvaren," Valyn teased as she withdrew from his arms.

"Get out of here." He shooed her away.

She chuckled as she scooped up the satchel and strapped a long-knife to her thigh. With one final look at him, she vaulted into the forest, disappearing into the darkness.

He was alone again. Alone with his thoughts, his memories, and the gentle hum of the life of the forest, but no hum of minds from the spire. He glanced up at the tree that held the sigil and sighed, content.

This was where he wanted to be.

E p i l o g u e

Theren had a vague sense that weeks had passed, though he wasn't counting. The sun rose and fell, the moon followed, and the stars wheeled in a predictable pattern above him. With the amulet tied under his glove against the skin of his wrist, he could relax his mind with no fear of detection. He slept soundly at night in a makeshift shelter in the trees and napped at times during the day. His sleep was silent, void of Dreams, and the urgent, unsettled feeling in his stomach had eased. He sometimes checked the sigil in the tree, which never changed. Visiting it took on a ritual-like quality; he might be disconnected from the spire now, but he held his forgotten ancestors in reverence. As Athas had said, there was so much about their history that was forgotten. With the destruction of the Void, a whole part of Alvar culture was no longer needed. Who knew what purpose the sigil served in the days of war? When Theren placed his hand over it, he imagined the hand of someone a thousand years past who had done the same.

He had mostly adjusted to life with such little Light within him; his body was still easily fatigued but he had enough energy to get by. Besides hunting the occasional creature for his dinner or foraging food from the abundant forest, he had little to occupy his time. He filled his days by sitting in the branches and looking out over the fields of waving green grass, sun-season's warm breezes caressing his skin.

It was one such warm day when Theren sat on his usual branch, gazing out over a clear, blue day. The broken spire, a shattered relic of an age long-lost, shimmered behind the heat of the midday sun. Theren leaned against the trunk of the tree and let a leg overhang the branch, kicking it lazily in the warm air. He was barefooted, his gloves discarded in the campsite. His shirt was open, the dim ithlyn on his chest almost invisible in the bright sunlight.

"It's a beautiful day," he said to himself, his eyes feeling heavy in the heat. He thought of Valyn and wondered where she was. Though part of him worried about her, he felt distant, as though the feeling belonged in another life. She was in charge of her own fate now. Nothing seemed to worry him much anymore, save his sleepy vigil at the edge of the forest. He closed his eyes and smiled.

When he opened them again, he was not sure whether he was awake, for he saw movement in the distance, silhouetted against the setting sun. On the hills past the broken spire, shadows moved through the long grass.

Theren shot to his feet, gripping the tree to lean out for a better look. His heart hammered loudly in his chest. He peered out over the valley. Closer and closer the shadows came, breaking off into small groups, moving around the ruins of the broken spire. They were not shadows, he realised. They were figures.

People?

He knew, then, he must be Dreaming.

"Ena, am I awake?" he whispered. Of course, there was no reply.

He watched, frozen, waiting for the figures to approach the forest. Perhaps they were men from another spire who had decided, for some reason, to cross the open fields of the Abyss rather than stick to the forests? It was an unlikely notion, and Theren dismissed it as the figures milled around the ruins. They were not coming his way.

Was this Dream a memory? A foretelling? He waited for a feeling, for some sign from Ena that would help him understand. Nothing came.

"When will I wake up?" he asked aloud. He huddled against the trunk of his tree. His bare hands gripped the bark. The sun continued sinking slowly towards the horizon. Smoke from several small fires began to drift into the air from within the ruins. Occasionally, he could spot the figures on the walls.

Questions raced through his mind as he watched. What were they? Was this a memory of the Void? But, if it were, why was the spire in the field still broken? He waited as the sun set, a sinking feeling in his stomach.

"Wake up, wake up, wake up." He clutched his head.

There was no denying it now. The Dreamers' madness had claimed him. He was trapped in a Dream and he was not able to shake it.

It had to be a Dream. Or perhaps a hallucination. This was not real.

No one lived in the Abyss.

Author's Note

Dear reader

Thank you for being here! I am so grateful for the time you have taken to read my book.

All of my fantasy stories are set in the world of Ahira, at various points in history. The Dreamer can be considered something of a 'supplementary' work to my main series, *The Offered*, the first book of which is coming out in October 2023.

To find out more about me or my books, please head to www.jeanswan.com or find me on Twitter and Instagram under @jeanswanauthor, or on TikTok at @jean_swan. I am always keen to chat!

Finally — if you liked this book, please consider rating or leaving a review on Goodreads, Amazon, or wherever you like to review. Your support helps indie authors more than you can imagine!

Thank you again
Jean

A c k n o w l e d g e m e n t s

To my lovely readers who take the time to
message me or write a review — thank you,
thank you, thank you!
Your words of support mean so much, and
I love sharing my stories with you.

To my ever-patient first readers, editors, and
sounding boards, Kelly and Josh. Your brains
are my greatest writing tool and I cannot ever
thank you enough for your support.

To my little brother, Mikey, for the nights
reading our stories to each other and your
calm co-existence on writing days.

To my editor, Katie-bree Reeves for your thoughtful edits and labouring over proper nouns, hyphens, and italics with me!

To my parents, for reading to me every night as a little one. To both my grandparents for taking us on adventures that inspired many stories, and — especially — Grandma: I borrowed your name and inherited your love of whimsy and wonder.

About the Author

Jean lives in south-eastern Australia, with her dog and husband. When not writing or working, you'll find her anywhere there's beach or snow, hanging with her gang of nieces and godchildren, or in the garden trying to stay on top of the weeds. And reading, of course!

Forthcoming Books

The Book of Origins (Book One of *The Offered)*

*"A dakir is the silent knife in the night,
the eyes everywhere, that will do what no other can
or will in service to the Nexus."*

An authoritarian empire.
A mysterious new land.
Whispers of rebellion.

And three young spies
who have to make sense of it all.

www.ingramcontent.com/pod-product-compliance
Lightning Source LLC
Chambersburg PA
CBHW020354120726
47904CB00002B/556